WYRDE AND WICKED

HOUSE OF WERTH: 2

CHARLOTTE E. ENGLISH

ONE

Disappointing as it may be to relate the state of dullness prevailing at Werth Towers after the exciting events of the summer, yet it must be done. This, after all, is an endeavour prizing Truth over fashion.

Overflowing with the enthusiasm attending a series of mild successes, then (for so we will term such a succession of catastrophes, on the grounds that they *could* have turned out a great deal worse), Gussie would have attacked the matter of the Books with gusto. Indeed, she tried.

She began by turning her uncle's library upside down, much to the disgust of a bristling Lord Bedgberry.

'Really, Gussie!' said he, having wandered, in a state only half-awake, into this favourite part of the house, with a view to changing his copy of *A Natural History of Lycanthropes* for some new, exciting treatise. 'What can you mean by all this mess?'

His lordship's expostulations were not unjust. Gussie (and her faithful Miss Frostell) had soon tired of removing a single book at a time, carefully checking its title page and contents, before neatly returning it to the shelf. Gussie's urgent curiosity and Miss Frostell's boundless enthusiasm would not admit of so slow a pace. Inevitably, then, the ladies soon fell to removing the leather-bound books by the armful, and discarding the greater part upon the nearby tables, and soon after upon the floor.

'Help us, then,' said Gussie impatiently, barely attending to Theo's dismay. 'With the three of us at work, we shall soon have checked every book.'

'For what, pray?' said Theo, not moving from his station in the doorway. Gussie, casting a careless glance in his direction, observed that he existed in a state of high indignation, from the toes of his shoes to the tips of his rusty-hued hair. Indeed, the latter appeared almost to be standing on end with horror.

'For something pertaining to those wretched Books,' said Gussie, returning, unfazed, to her ransacking of the shelves. 'There must be something among all these tomes, I am sure of it.'

There were indeed a great number of volumes crowded into Lord Werth's library, successive generations of the family having frequently boasted a Theo among them (that being, a learned gentleman of bookish habits; his other predilections being not nearly so common, even among the Werths). 'I cannot be the first of the family to entertain a lively curiosity about the Book of Werth,' said Gussie hopefully. 'Even if its fellows in bookish iniquity were hitherto unknown.'

'Were they, though?' put in Miss Frostell, presently engaged in hefting quite ten or twelve burdensome volumes in her arms all at once. Her destination was the deep window-seat, through which the afternoon sun shone golden and inviting (and ignored). As she spoke, one hapless tome slithered from her uncertain grasp, and fell to the floor with a *bang*.

Theo started forward. 'Careful! Dash it, these books are valuable!'

'That is a good notion, Frosty,' said Gussie, ignoring Theo (as she so often did). 'Perhaps some forebear of ours *did* know of the other Books, and the fact has simply been forgotten!' Upon which encouraging reflection, she renewed her attack upon the shelves.

'Book, Gussie,' said Theo, occupying himself with an attempt to restore some of the books to their shelves (fruitless, for his efforts were easily outmatched by the ladies). 'We know of only *one* other Book.'

'If there is a second, I am persuaded there is a third,' said Gussie, her words emerging half muffled, for she had thrust her head into the deep recess of a shelf in quest of a slim volume that had fallen down the back. 'Perhaps rather more. And since both Books have shown a propensity to lie dormant for months at a time, or even years, well! They could be everywhere.'

'Let us hope not,' said Theo fervently.

'I am hoping *so*,' Gussie retorted. 'To conduct a properly scientific study, we require more specimens. The more, the merrier! And I should like very much to know which of the Wyrded families of the country possess such a Book as ours.'

'The Selwyns do not,' Miss Frostell reminded her erstwhile charge.

'No, that is true. But that does not necessarily mean that they never had one, does it?'

'Do you mean that they may have lost it?' said Miss Frostell.

'Precisely. This second Book has obviously entered the book trade, at one point or another in its life. Other such tomes may have been sold, or even stolen away from their original owners.'

'I should like to know where you imagine you are going with this line of thinking,' said Theo, abandoning his attempts to restore order, and sinking hopelessly into the welcoming arms of a deep library-chair. 'I find it impossible to follow it.'

'I hardly know myself,' admitted Gussie. 'I believe we are speculating.'

'Speculating,' uttered Theo in disgust. 'No amount of

speculation will uncover *facts*, Gussie.'

'But we have so few facts to work with. Hardly any at all. I must, then, have something else to amuse me.'

Theo gave a great sigh, and rested his face in his hands. 'You will not find anything of use in here,' he said into his palms. 'I should be very surprised if anyone has discovered enough about the Book of Werth to write about it.'

'Whyever not?' said Gussie. 'When it has been in our possession for such a great many years—'

'Yes, and everyone with any sense at all has kept well clear of it, except at need.'

Gussie, mindful of her own visit to the Book not long ago, with Lady Werth for company, said with unimpaired cheer: 'Well, and I never was accused of possessing a great deal of sense. I had never before thought such a lack might stand me in good stead, but so it proves! I am the perfect person to investigate.'

'And so am I!' said Miss Frostell gaily, hurling another stack of tomes onto the floor. A choking cloud of dust arose, sending her into a fit of coughing.

'Help us, Theo!' Gussie ordered, but to no avail, for her cousin would not be persuaded.

And the sad truth is that his nay-saying lordship was perfectly correct. Not a single clue as to the Book's history or nature did Gussie find in her uncle's library, not even among the forgotten tomes gathering dust in the neglected corners. She and her eager co-investigator were obliged to seek an alternative avenue for discovery.

'I shall write to Mrs. Daventry,' Gussie announced, a week or so later. 'Doubtless she will have more to tell us regarding the history of her curse-book. And my uncle could hardly object to my corresponding with so respectable a female, I am sure?'

'Most certainly he could not!' said Miss Frostell (really, the most obliging of companions, being always as enthused about Gussie's projects as Gussie could be herself). 'I shall fetch your writing-desk, my dear, for I am sure you will want to begin directly.'

The writing-desk was accordingly brought; Gussie seated herself at a corner table in the parlour of her little cottage; and the letter was composed forthwith.

Any detail you may recall may be of the gravest importance, Gussie put in. *Anything at all, however small! I shall be most grateful to you!*

But disappointment was once again to be Gussie's lot, for when the reply came, after the passage of yet another week, it contained nothing but demurrals. The curse-book had been sold by a dealer in books, who had received it as part of a varied lot, of no particular distinction. Nothing of its provenance was known to Mrs. Daventry, nor had she received any hint as to its true nature before the events in which Miss Werth had already played a part. She had read the curse-book quite through, and it had behaved itself beautifully, made not the smallest attempt to maim her; a model of good breeding, if such could be said of a collection of pages bound in leather, and elegantly inscribed.

Gussie, cruelly disappointed, penned another letter, urging her to take up the banner of investigator, and chase after the book-dealer, for surely the man must know where he had got the "varied lot" containing the curse-book.

But to this, she received no response at all.

Autumn being by now some way advanced, Gussie's spirits sank along with the sun. Her uncle had banned any further visits to either Book, upon pain of immediate dismemberment. Whenever Gussie felt tempted to flout this command (which, she had to own, was not an unreasonable one), she recalled the thunderous look adopted by Lord Werth as he had laid down this stricture, and felt that he might have meant the threat more literally than she would like.

'Though perhaps I could spare a limb,' she reflected to Miss Frostell, upon one especially dull evening. Marooned as she was in her snug parlour, with only a single candle to chase away the gloom of the season, and obliged to fall back on her embroidery for employment, impatience gnawed at her until she could barely keep her seat. 'Not *any* limb, of course,' she said, in amendment of this happy thought. 'I should prefer to keep both of my legs, or I shall be quite the charge upon my family. I should have to be carried everywhere in a sedan chair.'

'The inconvenience would be considerable,' agreed Miss Frostell. 'And perhaps not *quite* worth the gain.'

'But my arms,' Gussie pursued. 'My right I might elect to keep, but my left? It is by far the less used of the two, and when you consider how little fancy-work I shall be able to attempt with only one hand, really I shall be quite the gainer.'

Miss Frostell, occupying a seat beside Gussie upon an elegant silken divan, cast an appraising look at Miss Werth's embroidery-frame. Its centre sported an exciting scene, near fully developed: the Book of Werth chased a hapless Lord Bedgberry with murderous intent, sprouting appendages from all four of its corners. Theo wore an expression of stark terror. Judging from the quantity of blood, he had already been divested of at least a couple of fingers.

'But it is a charming piece,' said Miss Frostell firmly. 'When it is finished I shall make a cushion of it. Your dear aunt would like it excessively, would not she?'

'I believe not, Frosty, for my aunt persists in holding Theo in affection.'

'Why, so do I! But dear Lord Bedgberry must soon come about. I am persuaded he is about to wreak a terrible vengeance upon the Book. Perhaps a second panel?'

'True, no hero worth his salt could be so poor-spirited as to mind a little maiming,' Gussie agreed. 'Excellent notion, Frosty. I shall persuade Theo to visit the Books. He shall interrogate them for us, and bring us the results. And if my uncle should feel disposed to inflict bodily harm over it, he shall turn his wrath upon Theo, and not us. Really, it is quite perfect.'

'I had not entirely—' began Miss Frostell, but to no avail, for Gussie was gone in a moment, pausing only to collect her bonnet and pelisse on her way out into the park. The hour may be late, and chill, but no true heroine could object to a little freezing in pursuit of the Truth; and Theo preferred the dark. She had always known that of him.

She wandered the grounds of Werth Towers for some time in search of her abominable cousin, who would, she knew, be out and prowling on so fine and crisp an evening. Her pursuit carried her down an avenue of ancient chestnut trees, a favourite with Lady Werth; over a succession of hillocks and meadows, daringly attempted in the weak light of a half-moon; and finally ended in the very glade, with its stone altar, in which Lord Felix had so iniquitously summoned a plethora of distant family connections not so long ago. (And the deleterious effects of his ridiculous ritual were still being felt, for once in a while a stranger still arrived at the Towers, citing a compulsion to travel to the house, and demanding to know What The Matter Was. Lord and Lady Werth had yet to find any of them of much interest).

The glade, dark and a trifle eerie even in the golden summer, was positively brooding at night. Thus Gussie felt no surprise at all upon finding Theo there, seated upon the altar, and apparently lost in thought.

'Your hind-quarters must be frozen to the bone,' Gussie commented, ducking her head to avoid the low-hanging branches of a gnarly yew tree.

'The state of my hind-quarters, now or at any other time, can hardly be said to be any of your business,' Theo retorted.

'And when they are frozen square and you cannot walk, I shall of course be overpowered with sympathy.'

Theo merely grunted.

'I am come with an entreaty,' Gussie persevered.

'No doubt. And you should not be here at all at this hour, especially unaccompanied, but *that* will not weigh with you.'

'Why should I not be? You can hardly imagine me to be in any danger in my uncle's own park.'

'No,' said Theo, with some regret. 'I suppose not.'

'Unless you are referring to Lord Maundevyle, but I *think* he likes me well enough not to maul me to death.'

'Not to death, at any rate. He might maul you a little, if you were to chatter at him in this same tiresome fashion.'

'He might!' Gussie allowed. 'Taciturn men are always discomposed whenever anybody speaks to them. I shall have to bear it in mind.'

'He is not here, however,' said Theo. 'I passed him in the lavender-grove an hour ago.'

Lord Maundevyle, in dragon-shape, had long displayed a peculiar fondness for Lady Werth's lavender bushes. He had taken refuge there, when his dejection over his enforced Wyrding had, for a time, overpowered his reason. Even now, having grown accustomed to his draconic form, he was still known to appear in the breakfast-room (human in shape, of course), redolent of lavender, and smiling. (Well, *almost* smiling).

Gussie could not account for it, but it was among his lordship's least objectionable habits.

'I need you to interrogate the Books for me,' said Gussie, impatient with these asides.

'No.'

'I cannot find out anything about them by any other means within my reach. But surely *they* must know something of their own history.'

'No,' said Theo again.

'Please, cousin,' said Gussie, despising herself as she spoke, for it never did to beg; it set men up in their own conceit, and encouraged them to imagine themselves important. But a desperate situation called for desperate measures.

'No!' growled Theo. 'My father has forbidden it, and for excellent reason. I will not go near either of those detestable Books.'

'But you manage them so beautifully—'

'The point is, I would far rather not have to manage them beautifully.'

'But—'

'No, Gussie. They are dangerous. *Truly* dangerous, not in a funning way. Why, one of them has killed a man! More than one! You saw the body with your own eyes. Would you like me to end up like that poor library-fellow?'

Gussie gave the matter due consideration. 'It *would* afford me a deal of pleasure,' she allowed. 'But I quite see that it would be unreasonable of me to expect such a sacrifice on your part.'

'And if,' continued Theo, ignoring this, 'you are minded to attempt an interrogation yourself, allow me to inform you that the Books are under constant watch. My father's orders. If you are seen to so much as venture down the stairs, a report will go to my uncle immediately, and you will be detained by any means available.'

Gussie scoffed. 'And who is it that could claim to reach my uncle so quickly? I should have plenty of time to get into the room, and by then, you know, it would be too late.'

'Great-Uncle Silvester,' said Theo.

That silenced Gussie. The grotesque, whose stone form her ancestor was presently haunting, could indeed be very quick when it suited him. He had wings, after all, and was capable of employing them. And if he had set himself against the idea of Gussie's reading the Books, then her options were much diminished.

'Even you cannot truly wish to endanger yourself out of mere curiosity,' Theo said.

'*Even* me?' Gussie answered. 'Why, am I so crack-brained as that?'

'Much more so.'

Gussie sighed. If she were to own the truth — and nothing could persuade her to do so aloud — then she had not quite the degree of inclination she professed. She had not, in fact, forgotten the sight of poor Mr. Fletcher, lying dead upon the floor of his own circulating library, his bloodied corpse savagely mauled. Nor had she forgotten the family Book's own iniquities, including so severe an injury to her uncle's hand as to leave him without the use of it for some weeks. She had little wish to try her own luck with the thing, or with Mrs. Daventry's murderous curse-book.

But nor could she consent to leave the matter unexplored.

'It is not merely a matter of curiosity,' she said. 'Those Books *are* dangerous. And what if there are more, Theo? What if Mrs. Daventry's is not the only such monster to have fallen into the hands of those ill-equipped to manage them?'

'That is not our concern,' said Theo shortly.

'No, but it should be.'

Theo rubbed at his eyes. 'Why, pray?'

'We may not know exactly what they are, or where they came from. But we are used to dealing with such things, and we have proved capable of confining them suitably. Is there any other family in the country who could say the same? Even Mr. Ballantine's Bow Street fellows could not.'

'In point of fact,' said Theo. 'I don't know.'

'There, then!' said Gussie, delighted. 'If you will not venture to visit the Books, will you at least make some enquiries among your cronies? Perhaps somebody has heard of another family like ours, in possession of just such another Book.'

'My cronies?' echoed Theo blankly.

'Why, yes, your friends and connections—'

'What in the world leads you to imagine that I *have* friends and connections?'

'I hear forever of gentlemen's clubs, where a great deal of inconsequent talk goes on—'

'Perhaps in London, Gussie. But in the back end of Norfolk? No. And when have you ever known me to venture so far as London?'

Gussie was silenced.

Theo rose from his chilly perch with a sigh, and stretched his long limbs. 'I will talk to my father,' he conceded. 'Perhaps he, or my mother, may have some of these "connections" you speak of, and will not mind consulting them.'

And so Gussie went away filled, once again, with hope.

But she was once again doomed to disappointment, for the rest of the autumn wore away, and winter set in; and if either her aunt or her uncle had acted upon Theo's suggestion with any success, Gussie did not hear of it.

Two

Never given to much in the way of compunction, Theo surprised himself by suffering a degree of guilt over his wilful deception of his cousin.

For deception it had been.

His guilt was not much to discompose him; the merest trifle; but he had lied directly to her face, and that face — smiling and eager, and professing opinions which, in some cases, he shared himself — occasionally rose in his memory.

He was *almost* tempted to apologise to it, when it did.

The facts were, that Theo was as alive as Gussie could be to the problems posed by the Books. Mrs. Daventry's currently reposed in his father's cellars because there had been nothing else to do with it. The thing must be confined, and if Ballantine had not been able to assume responsibility for it, then that duty fell to the Werths.

But that it posed a threat to his family, Theo could not deny.

Worst of all, he was afraid the Books... encouraged one another.

There were further facts he had concealed from Gussie (out of concern for her safety, he told himself, though his irritation with her overpowering enthusiasm might have

12

had something to do with it).

When he had declared he would not, under any circumstances, go anywhere near those Books, that had been a lie from start to finish.

For Theo frequently went near the Books. Every night, in fact. Before he set forth into the darkened grounds of the Towers for his usual nightly predations, he journeyed first into the cellars, taking one of his father's expensive gas-lamps with him (quite as though the bright and steady light might somehow protect him from *those things*).

He went first to the stout room in which the Book of Werth was confined, though he did not go inside. He only stood at the door, with his ear to the heavy oak boards, and listened.

Sometimes he heard the violent rattling of a table, as though the Book were thrashing about; a bookish equivalent of stamping around in a fury, he supposed.

And sometimes he heard it whispering. Long strings of dulcet, incomprehensible mutterings, barely audible through the thick door, but chilling enough for all that, for Theo had no difficulty in understanding to whom it spoke.

It spoke to Mrs. Daventry's curse-book.

The second Book lay imprisoned in a neighbouring cellar-room. Theo had not preferred it that way, but the cellars were not so expansive as all that; only one room had the stout walls and thick door he considered necessary to keep it safely locked away. At first he had cherished some hopes that the damage Lord Maundevyle's dragon-teeth had done to the thing might have overpowered it forever; that it might, to use a common parlance, be dead. But he had not had the faith to rely upon it, and in this at least he had been proved wise.

For when the Book of Werth whispered its dark mutterings to the curse-book, the curse-book whispered back.

It did not seem to matter what time of night he arrived to listen, either. On one occasion, he had not made his nightly visit until dawn was on the point of breaking. Even then, the whisperings continued.

Either the wretched things waited until he was present to talk to one another, or they were engaged in such lengthy discourse as to require all the night-time hours in which to do it. Only when the sun was up did they at last fall silent.

As soon as he had established these facts beyond the possibility of doubt, Theo had dispatched the news to Mr. Ballantine at Bow Street. And he had received a prompt reply, but it had no power to soothe his disquiet.

What you say is greatly concerning, Mr. Ballantine had written. *I wish I had something to tell you, or to do for you, that would prove to be of use, but I find myself powerless. I have not been able to discover anything new about either of the books, nor have I heard of any more such creatures.*

If at any time it should be possible for you to discern what they are whispering about, *I should be most interested to hear of it.*

Theo had tried, and it was an experience he had no wish to repeat. He had gone in to visit the Book of Werth, taking with him his hatchet. Not only had he immediately got into a violent altercation, but he had heard nothing of use, for his arrival had put an end to the whisperings altogether.

He had gone away, victorious but bleeding, and nothing the wiser.

'It seems that they are no longer inclined to turn quiescent,' said Theo to his father, a week or two after the conversation with Gussie which has already been related. 'Presumably each is too much encouraged by the presence of the other to return into dormancy.'

He had answered a summons from Lord Werth, and found him ensconced in his own book-room. The space was small and comfortable, containing only those few volumes Lord Werth particularly prized, and fitted otherwise with a quantity of deep arm-chairs, bright lamps, and blazing fires.

Lord Werth, positioned before a roaring blaze, but with no book before him, regarded his son in silent thought. Theo read concern in his face. 'I must own, I wish we did not have to give house-room to that second Book,' he said.

'I wish it too, and I should like to wring Lord Felix's neck,' said Theo. 'Were it not for his damned ritual, we would never have known Ballantine, and we would have known nothing of Mrs. Daventry's Book either.'

'It would, then, have been someone else's problem?' said Lord Werth, with a faint smile.

'I do not see why it has to be our problem,' said Theo bluntly. 'Only it has become so, and we must manage it as best we may.'

'Quite so.' Lord Werth fell into an abstraction, staring into the leaping flames. 'Ballantine has no intention of removing it?' he finally said.

'He has said nothing of it. I suppose he could at any time, were it simply a matter of finding a stout room in which to imprison the thing. But no one at Bow Street has any experience of these Books, nor any idea of how to subdue them. I must own, it is nowhere as safe as it is here.'

'Safe,' sighed Lord Werth. 'You know, when I was a boy there were tales of the Book of Werth's past misdemeanours. I thought them greatly exaggerated. But perhaps they are not; and *if* they are not, then it has had periods of violence rivalling those of the curse-book.'

'Honoria declares there was once a Bertha,' said Theo. 'And Bertha came a cropper thanks to the Book.'

Lord Werth nodded.

'You have heard nothing of any other such Books?' Theo asked, mindful of Gussie's request.

'Not a thing.'

Theo took a deep breath. 'Then I have but one idea as to how to proceed.'

Lord Werth directed a look of enquiry at his son. His

face, with one brow slightly raised, and a gleam of resigned amusement in his eye, suggested he was fully aware how little he would like Theo's idea.

'It appears the origins of those Books have been forgotten,' Theo ventured. 'If we would like to know more of them, then we ought to consult those who came before.' He paused, and added, 'Long before.'

Lord Werth was heard to sigh. 'And I have but just got Lord Felix to stop clambering out of his grave every other morning.'

'It need not absolutely be Lord Felix?'

'Who else might you suggest? With all his faults, few are so well acquainted with the family's history as Felix. Besides, he has already shown signs of a greater familiarity with the Book and its ways than anybody living. He knew to find the ritual within its pages, after all, and he spoke of its tendency to conceal things.'

Theo nodded. 'Will you consult him, Father? I am persuaded that we cannot ignore the problems these Books present. And what's more, while I have firmly depressed the idea in Gussie's presence, I should not be at all surprised if there are more of them somewhere.'

Lord Werth winced. 'Let us all hope you are wrong.'

Theo's next errand took him into Lord Maundevyle's presence, though in this he found himself forestalled. Gussie sat in his mother's lavender-bower, charmingly attired in a periwinkle-blue pelisse and a bonnet with matching ribbons. She sat directly by Lord Maundevyle's head, for he, in his dragon form, lay prone among the bushes. There had grown up a dragon-shaped depression between the withering lavender, where he so often reposed himself.

'And have you heard from your mother so lately?' Gussie was saying, blithely unconcerned with the light drizzle of rain falling. 'I trust she is well.' This last was said with that look of bright-eyed mischief so common in her;

she trusted nothing of the kind, and took an unholy pleasure in her ladyship's probable discomposure.

'She informs me she has almost completed the repairs to the house,' rumbled Lord Maundevyle. 'The damage I effected with my "clumsy departure" is almost healed.'

'You are to be felicitated.' She looked up at Theo and smiled. 'Did you hear that, Theo? Lord Maundevyle's mother has been so clever as to find out his hiding-place. And she has *not* descended upon us in a fury! I believe we, too, are to be felicitated.'

'It can only be a matter of time,' said Theo darkly. 'She'll be here, with those other two unconscionable brats in her train.'

'How impolite,' murmured Gussie. 'You ought not to describe our guest's siblings as brats, Theo.'

Theo shrugged his shoulders.

'Hellions, perhaps,' she continued. 'Criminals in the making, bound to be taken up by the constable at any moment. But they must have left the condition of *brat* behind years ago.'

'Not in Clarissa's case,' said Lord Maundevyle.

'I concede the point,' said Gussie.

'Delightful as these little asides are,' growled Theo. 'I came here with something particular to say, if I may have your attention?'

'Why, certainly!' Gussie gave him her brightest smile. 'We have been unimaginably dull without you.'

Theo frowned at her, and turned his attention to the dragon. 'Lord Maundevyle, I come with an entreaty. It's to do with those dratted Books.'

'If you are about to ask me to go in search of Lady Margery, you are behind the fair,' said his lordship.

Gussie, Theo realised, was positively beaming at him. 'I have already asked him! And it was a very good notion, was it not?'

'Quite brilliant,' Theo said. 'May I enquire as to whether his lordship is planning to leave anytime this year,

17

or must it wait until after Christmas?'

'Bravo, Theo!' Gussie saluted him. 'A sally worthy of my own tongue.'

Lord Maundevyle hauled himself a little upright, blowing desiccated fronds of lavender over the rain-slick path. 'And how, pray, do either of you propose I should discover Lady Margery's whereabouts?'

Gussie made some incomprehensible gesture with her hands. A shooing motion, though with some quirk to it suggestive of mystique. 'Have you no dragon senses to employ?'

'Had I any, before?' said Lord Maundevyle pointedly.

'No, but you are now so much more comfortable in your dragon-shape, are not you? I quite thought you might have some new ability at your disposal.'

'Nothing of the sort,' said his lordship shortly.

'How lowering.'

'Though having made her ladyship's acquaintance, I believe I may have one idea…' said Lord Maundevyle. 'I collect the matter is urgent.'

'I fear it is,' said Theo.

Gussie gasped. 'And when you had so determinedly suppressed its importance to me!'

'Because I knew you would interfere if I did not, but I can see that no words of mine can discourage you from doing so.'

'I do not see why I should not "interfere", if you are going to,' said Gussie, rising from her own seat upon a low stone bench. 'What's more, I have *another* excellent notion.'

Theo, conscious of feelings of foreboding, directed a quelling frown at his cousin. Predictably, this had no effect whatsoever. 'And what is this notion?'

'It appears we are thinking along similar lines,' she said. 'If nobody living knows anything about the Books, and there are no written records of them to be found, why then we must consult our ancestors.'

'My father is already going to speak with Lord Felix,'

said Theo quickly. 'You can leave that one alone.'

She blinked at him in surprise, and possibly horror. 'No, Theo! We cannot have that ritual conducted again! Not if we were plagued by a hundred Books.'

'No, no,' he hastened to say. 'That isn't the idea at all, and I am not at all persuaded that it would be of the least use anyway. I merely want to find out what he knows.'

'Oh! That will be acceptable, of course.' She made a curtsey to Lord Maundevyle, and turned back toward the house. 'Good journey, your lordship!' she called over her shoulder.

Theo made his own, hasty goodbyes, before falling into step beside Gussie. 'You haven't told me what the notion is. Quickly, please, before I perish of heart failure.'

'I am going to my aunt and uncle,' said Gussie, walking with a brisk pace towards the house. 'I should like to have their permission to invite Nell for a visit.'

'She has not visited enough of late?'

'Honestly, Theo, can you feel affection for nobody?'

'I have affection enough for your sister, but—'

'In that case you will be delighted to welcome her back to the Towers,' said Gussie firmly. 'Particularly since she can speak to some of the long-dead Werths who lie beyond my uncle's reach.'

Theo was silent from a mixture of admiration and chagrin.

'Hah!' crowed Gussie. 'You did not think of that, did you?'

Theo did not like to admit how infrequently he thought of Nell in general. She had married young, and left the Towers so long ago as to have fallen quite out of his thoughts. 'It is a good notion,' he forced himself to say, though the words of praise near stuck in his throat.

Gussie contented herself with a silent glow of satisfaction, and refrained from gloating further.

Which was most unlike her. 'Is there anything else you're planning?' he said, suspicions aroused.

'Not immediately.'

'At some later date?'

'I will tell you about it,' Gussie allowed.

'*Thank you.*'

'At some later date.'

A growl escaped Theo's throat.

Gussie, arrived at the side-door into the house, paused to flash Theo a bright smile. 'It sounds time for your repast, dear cousin. Do not let hunger get the better of you, pray, or we shall all be in the basket.'

Theo stalked away, leaving her to let herself into the house. Much as it galled him, she was perfectly right; he was famished, and his frustrations would be much better worked out in pursuit of a meal.

Three

In point of fact, Gussie had two requests to put before her uncle and aunt, only one of which she had shared with Theo.

It was the work of a mere few minutes to procure a sufficient invitation for Nell.

'Why, of course,' said Lady Werth, having been run to earth in the dining-parlour, brightening a bouquet of hothouse flowers. 'We are always delighted to see dear Nell.'

Gussie, finding it prudent not to mention her real reason for desiring Nell's company, permitted her aunt to imagine her missing her sister. Which was perfectly true, after all.

'And there is another matter for which I should like your permission, Aunt.'

Lady Werth, as alive as her son to signs of danger from Gussie, looked up, and subjected her niece to a narrow-eyed look. 'And what is that?'

'It's to do with my Wyrde.'

'I see.'

For Gussie had not forgotten the matter of her own condition, despite her preoccupation with the Books. 'I have hit upon an excellent idea,' she said. 'A way of finding out more about it, while also making some enquiries on my uncle's behalf regarding the Books.'

'I believe your uncle forbade you to do anything of the kind?' said Lady Werth, without much hope of making an impression.

'Only because he did not want me to endanger myself, and I have no such intention, of course.'

'Of course,' said her ladyship faintly.

'I would like to see Lady Maundevyle,' said Gussie.

'That mad woman? No!' Lady Werth set down her scissors with a clatter, dropping a few roses in her dismay.

'It may be done here, if you should like me not to go to Starminster,' Gussie said quickly. 'And then you may keep an eye on her.'

Lady Werth appeared to be bereft of words.

'I only want to ask her some questions,' said Gussie. 'Her family used to be among the most Wyrded in England, did it not? Well, I want to know if they ever possessed such a Book as ours.'

'And how is this related to your Wyrde?' said Lady Werth.

'It isn't, of course. *That* is quite a simple matter,' said Gussie. 'I am going to Wyrde her.'

'I do not believe I have ever heard the word used as a verb in quite that fashion.'

'No, it is my own invention,' said Gussie modestly.

Lady Werth, overpowered by her emotions, sank into the nearest of her elegant dining-chairs. 'Perhaps you had better explain the whole plan to me.'

Gussie took a seat next to her aunt. 'It is quite simple,' she began. 'I would like to gather more information, of course. If her ladyship proves to be, as yet, unWyrded — which may *not* be the case, or why has she not descended upon us with further demands upon me? — well, I can cautiously conclude that mere proximity to me is insufficient to effect the change. And if a person must be touched in order to be changed by me, naturally that is what I would next plan to do.'

'To make sense of this convoluted explanation,' said her aunt. 'If Lady Maundevyle has not already succumbed to a Wyrding curse, you propose to bestow one upon her forthwith?'

'Exactly!'

'I suppose it would be useless to present my objections?'

'I can hardly see how there could be any,' Gussie said. 'I should not wander about Wyrding people willy-nilly, of course; you are perfectly right about that. But where can be the harm in testing my capabilities upon someone who has positively begged me to do it? I admit I am annoyed with myself for not doing it before, when I had the chance. I believe I was angry.'

'And his lordship had just destroyed half of the house, which I imagine must distract anybody just a little,' said Lady Werth.

'Quite so. Well, I am surprised we have not already had her driving up to the Towers and kicking up a fuss. It seems all too likely that we *shall*, in due time, especially now that she has finished repairing Starminster.'

'Oh, has she?' faintly echoed Lady Werth.

'Oh yes, it is quite mended. Lord Maundevyle, as you may imagine, was delighted with the news.'

'Was he really?'

'I am almost sure of it. It is difficult to be certain. The deciphering of draconic facial expressions is not among my talents.'

'The product of a lack of experience only,' said Lady Werth. 'You will soon come about, if we are to have him forever haunting the shrubbery.'

'So I may invite her?' Gussie pursued.

Lady Werth sat up with a look of alarm. 'No! Not *here*. Gussie, recall the damage done to Starminster! If we are to have half the Towers pulled down, your uncle will never forgive us.'

'We could do it outside? Then, if she is to be a dragon like her son, there will be no harm done.'

Lady Werth regarded her niece with wide-eyed horror. 'I perceive you are perfectly serious.'

'Why, yes,' said Gussie in surprise. 'This is not something to be funning about.'

'When in general, everything is,' murmured her aunt.

'So may I—'

Lady Werth held up a hand. 'I must think it over, and I must of course consult your uncle.'

'It really will be the best way to go about it,' said Gussie in her most persuasive tone.

And Lady Werth sighed. 'The worst of it is, I suspect you may be right.'

The results of Lady Werth's conversation with her husband were delivered to Gussie by way of a severed head.

Two days after her hopeful entreaty to her aunt, Gussie lingered over the breakfast table with Miss Frostell, devoting herself to a plate of toast. Her thoughts were far away, her gaze fixed upon some indistinct point out of the window. Her great-aunt Honoria's appearance, therefore, took her by surprise.

'And have you really talked Georgiana into inviting that madwoman to the Towers?' said she without preamble, manifesting with a *pop* some three feet above the breakfast table.

A startled Gussie, regarding with dismay the upside-down morsel of toast now adorning the table-cloth, gave a sigh. 'Could not you contrive to announce yourself?' she said. 'As delightful as it is to see you, Aunt, I should appreciate a warning. Something charming, by preference.'

'A flurry of ethereal bells,' said Miss Frostell dreamily.

'Not in my line,' said Great-Aunt Honoria.

'No doubt you'd prefer a scream of terror,' said Gussie sourly. 'Or better yet, a chorus of them.'

Great-Aunt Honoria's smile might best be described as ghoulish. 'An excellent notion. What a fine revenant you will make, when the happy hour comes!'

'The happy hour of my death?' Gussie inquired. 'I am greatly looking forward to it, as you may imagine.'

'I have already arranged everything with your uncle,' said Honoria. 'He will have you out of your grave in a trice. Is that not generous of him? Though I am afraid your aunt has refused to entertain the notion of your thereafter being invited into the dining-parlour.'

'Which has never prevented *you*,' Gussie pointed out. 'Once dead, of course, I need not care for the proprieties anymore.'

Miss Frostell gave a diffident little cough. 'My dear, I feel bound to point out that you have never cared overmuch for the proprieties while living?'

'An unanswerable point,' Gussie conceded. 'My uncle merely humours you, however, Aunt. In the ordinary way of things he might be expected to predecease me, and I hope even *you* could not be so uncivil as to wish me an early death?'

'I had not thought of that,' said Honoria, crestfallen. 'Still,' she added, cheering in an instant, 'there is no saying but what there may be another with your uncle's Wyrde, in due course. If you should live to be an old lady, there is every chance of it.'

'A consoling reflection,' Gussie agreed. 'We have wandered away from the point, however, have we not? What did you mean, Aunt, about the madwoman?'

'Lady Maundevyle!' Great-Aunt Honoria's head bobbed furiously up and down, whether with excitement or indignation Gussie could not have said. 'Georgiana is to extend her an invitation!'

'To the Towers?'

'Yes! And I understand it is all your doing, Gussie! What *can* you have meant by it?'

'Why, I intend to find things out!' Gussie, energised,

attacked her breakfast with renewed vigour.

'How obliging of her ladyship!' said Miss Frostell, smiling.

'Is it not, though?' Gussie agreed. 'I was prepared for a refusal.'

'If you intend to find out whether or not Lady Maundevyle is mad, I am persuaded you need not go to half as much trouble,' said Honoria.

'Oh no,' Gussie agreed. 'There cannot be two opinions about *that*. What I would like to determine is whether or not she is Wyrded by now; what I may be able to do about it, if she is not; and whether her deplorable family ever had, say, a Book of Maundevyle.'

'Ohhh,' said Honoria, her eyes brightening. 'Such a Book must be more deranged even than ours.'

'If it is, I hope that it is lost because it was burned,' said Gussie.

'Burning,' mused Honoria. 'If we were to set the cellars alight, do not you think that would be an excellent solution?'

'A stroke of brilliance, except that I am afraid the rest of the house would likely be burned up along with the Books.'

'But it is a shabby old place,' said Honoria. 'A rebuilding would be just the thing.'

'I refer you to my uncle. If anybody is to authorise the burning down of the Towers, it must be he.'

'Quite right,' said Honoria. 'I will speak to him about it.'

'Whatever have you been doing, Aunt? You appear quite drowned in dust,' said Gussie. For while a quantity of cobwebs and dead spiders were commonly to be seen adorning Honoria's high-stacked, white-powdered hair, today's crop was especially abundant.

'When I declared the Towers to be a shabby old place, I spoke with the authority of recent experience,' said Honoria, and disappeared.

Gussie finished her toast.

'My dear,' said Miss Frostell. 'I congratulate you most sincerely, but I must own myself a little concerned about that woman's coming here. Are not you?'

'Very little. If she proves too great a nuisance, we will feed her to Theo, and there will be an end of it.'

'Dear Lord Bedgberry,' said Miss Frostell fondly.

FOUR

Gussie's first notice of Nell's arrival was the appearance of Aunt Margaret.

The sight of that industrious lady greeted Gussie upon her stepping into the great hall at the Towers one afternoon.

'Where is she taking all those linens?' Gussie said to Miss Frostell, who attended her. 'I must have seen her hauling those piles about any number of times.'

The two women watched in fascinated silence as the vision wafted from one side of the hall to the other. She had died in her fifties, by her appearance, for she moved with a brisk, efficient step, though her hair was fully grey. The voluminous skirts shrouding her portly figure proclaimed her to have lived some few decades before; her bowed posture implied a put-upon existence.

She had a kindness for Nell, Gussie supposed, for she appeared only when Mrs. Thannibour visited the Towers. Why she troubled to manifest at all, even Nell could not explain, for the majority of the resident spirits never did.

'Gussie!' came Nell's voice an instant later, and then came Nell herself. Her figure, fuller than Gussie's own, appeared to advantage in a new lace-trimmed gown, though its sober blue colour suited her status as a young matron.

'*Delightful* cap,' Gussie said, returning her sister's embrace.

Nell laughed, touching the froth of lace adorning her dark hair. 'Arthur declared it fetching, but I could not decide whether he was humouring me.' Then, pausing to listen to something Gussie could not hear, she added, 'No, no, Arthur is not by nature dishonest!'

'Then he is far superior to the generality of men,' Gussie said.

'You have no cause to be so cynical, Gus,' said Nell. 'No, she is *not* perfectly right!'

'Aunt Margaret?' Gussie guessed.

'No, poor Margaret is always so agreeable. It is Beatrice who has Opinions.'

Gussie felt at once that she might have liked Beatrice.

'Have you seen my aunt and uncle already?' said she.

'Yes, I have been sitting with them this half-hour.'

'Excellent; then we need not delay.' Gussie took her sister's arm and propelled her out of the hall. 'There is no time to lose!'

'Why, where are we going?' said Nell.

'To talk to every dead Werth we can get hold of.'

'Yes, I am come prepared to hold a conclave,' said Nell. 'But if you are minded to take me down into the cellars, I must entreat you to reconsider.'

'Oh,' said Gussie, and halted halfway down a white-walled passage leading straight to the cellar stairs. 'You do not wish it?'

'No, because it is perishingly cold down there.'

'But is it not true that the spirits are excessively fond of it?'

Nell looked at her as though she had run mad. 'Of course it is not. Why should they be?'

'I only thought...' Gussie felt her cheeks warm, and could not continue. She had been misled merely by the atmosphere down in the cellar rooms; as though a settled, damp chill and a gloomy lack of light had anything to do with hauntings!

'If they were not fond of it in life, they are no more comfortable there afterwards,' Nell said. 'And I cannot think what living person could possibly conceive a fondness for so dreary a place.'

'Then let us choose somewhere warmer, by all means. I should prefer it myself.'

'Your dear aunt's favourite parlour, perhaps?' suggested Miss Frostell.

'Undoubtedly the warmest room in the house, Frosty,' Gussie agreed. 'Though my aunt may object to the disturbance?'

'She may enjoy an opportunity to improve her acquaintance with my uncle's forebears,' said Nell, and turned her steps towards the parlour in question. The little group arrived to find not only Lady Werth in possession of the room, but Lord Werth as well. The two sat before the fire, with a third chair near at hand. The latter had been recently vacated by Nell, Gussie judged.

'Shall you object very much to our holding the conclave in here?' Nell said brightly, as she swept in.

'The conclave?' said Lady Werth, and turned accusing eyes on Gussie. 'I ought to have guessed!'

'In all probability, you ought rather,' Gussie agreed.

Lady Werth sighed. 'This is about the Books, I collect?'

'It is, and is it not a famous notion?' said Gussie. 'There is no telling who may be lurking about! And not every deceased Werth is to be found out in the churchyard, after all.'

'I should like to speak to Bertha,' said Lord Werth.

'Bertha?' echoed Nell.

'If she is to be found. It is Theo's idea that there was once someone of that name, and who was slain by the Book.'

'That is true,' said Gussie, struck by a fact that had, in

the recent confusion, slipped her mind. 'Was not it Honoria that said it?'

'I believe so.'

'Then it may have been a contemporary of hers. Nell, look for anyone of the last century.'

'That is not quite how it works,' said Nell drily, settling herself back into her warm chair before the fire. 'All I can do is issue an... invitation. Anyone who would like to join us will do so.'

'Very well, but can you at least issue a special invitation for Bertha?'

'I will do my best,' Nell promised.

Miss Frostell, as always a little awed by the dual presence of their lord and ladyships, took up a silent position at some distance from the fire. Gussie briefly entertained ideas of overriding this diffidence of hers, and hauling her nearer to the warmth; but it occurred to her that the governess might feel a degree of trepidation over the proceedings about to be entered into, and so she refrained. Not everyone preferred to be directly in the thick of things.

Nell sat quietly for a time, her eyes closed. She did not appear to be doing anything at all, and Gussie soon grew bored. How long did it take to summon all the dead generations of the House of Werth — or at least, those who still lingered around the Towers? Surely not so long! How her aunt and uncle could contrive to sit so still and patient, she could not fathom.

'Gussie,' said Lady Werth quietly. 'Pray do not fidget. You will distract Nell.'

Gussie controlled herself.

At long last, Nell opened her eyes. They had developed that odd haze over their customary grey-blue, an otherworldly sheen that appeared only when Nell exerted the deepest extent of her Wyrde. 'Uncle Thomas, is that you?' she said, smiling. 'And cousin Jane! Beatrice, of course I have not overlooked you. We are delighted to receive you. Aunt Margaret, perhaps you may pause in your labours for a little while, and join us in the parlour? Why, Great-Uncle Silvester! How well you look!'

This litany went on for some time, as Nell proceeded to greet a great many dead Werths. Gussie did not see Silvester's favourite grotesque anywhere; he had, then, opted to appear without it, at least for Nell. How intriguing. She wished she might see with Nell's eyes, just for a little while, for she might then look upon some vestige of his real face. That, and perceive the large gathering of dead relatives she understood to be manifesting around her.

'Mother,' said Nell, somewhere in the midst of her speech. 'Father. How we've missed you.'

This was not strictly true, or the plural was not. Nell, being some five or six years Gussie's senior, might have some remembrance of them, but they had died when Gussie was too small to know anything about it. Their absence from her life had not, therefore, troubled her overmuch; not when she had passed into the care of her capable aunt and uncle. Nonetheless, at these words of Nell's, her idle inclination to see these deceased family members for herself deepened into a hunger. In that moment, she would cheerfully have traded a great deal in exchange for Nell's Wyrde.

Nell held up a hand. 'I shall be delighted to speak to all of you at greater length a little later,' she said. 'But we are in conclave for a special purpose. Tell me, is there a Bertha present?'

Silence. Nell's face creased into a slight frown.

'Bertha has not come,' she said to Gussie. 'But some remember her. Beatrice says—' She stopped, and listened. 'Beatrice has much to say upon the subject,' she said quietly. 'It appears the name "Bertha" was used as a deterrent. If she would not stop spending so much time with the Book, she was told, she would end up torn to pieces, like her great-grandmother Bertha. Naturally, this

32

did not prevent her.'

Gussie sat up. 'The Book! Yes! We want to know everything about it.'

'*Was* she torn to pieces?' Lady Werth said in fascination. 'I remember a tale about Beatrice myself.'

'Very nearly,' said Nell. 'The thing behaved with great affection to her, she *says,* until one day when its embraces became positively lethal. She was fortunate to escape with her life.'

Gussie, remembering her last encounter with the Book of Werth, was moved to bless her own stars. She recalled being wound about with its clinging appendages, so tightly that she could not move. Nothing about its embrace had appeared to her as affectionate. Did that mean that Beatrice had misled herself, and wrongly interpreted its attentions? Or that it had treated Gussie with no such affection because, for her, it felt none?

'The Book can *feel*?' she said. 'It can be affectionate?'

Nell's eyes widened, and she once again held up a hand. 'One at a time, I beg you.'

Gussie waited in impatient silence.

'It is not held to be capable of anything remotely resembling affection,' Nell concluded after a time. 'Beatrice has been roundly ridiculed for suggesting it, I'm afraid. But she holds that it is, nonetheless, true. She and the Book dealt extremely well together, until the day its sentiments underwent some change.'

'Has it ever dispatched anybody else?' said Lord Werth.

'Not that I have heard today,' said Nell. 'But I can only reach those who have not been dead for so very long — perhaps not more than a century. Those who came before tend to be too far faded for conversation.'

'Nobody then would remember Lady Margery?' Gussie said.

Nell waited, listening, and finally shook her head. 'Stories only. No one here ever met her.'

'It was worth a try,' Gussie sighed. Whether or not they

received a further opportunity to consult the elderly dragon would depend upon Lord Maundevyle's efforts. She hoped his one idea for finding her proved to be a brilliant one.

'That means that Bertha is the only one of us to have died to the Book in a century,' mused Lord Werth.

'Rather more,' Nell said. 'Not forgetting that some of those here today *died* a century ago. Their lives, then, date still further back.'

Lord Werth nodded. 'And while it has had its periods of violence in recent memory, I would say it has in general been fairly well-behaved.'

Lady Werth agreed. 'Gussie and I ventured to visit it in reasonable safety, and I have done so several times in the past few years. It has hardly ever tried to harm me.'

'Until recently,' said Gussie. 'For it did try to harm *me*, and in just the fashion Beatrice experienced.' A thought struck her. 'Was not the same thing true of Mrs. Daventry's curse-book? It was altogether dormant, until a few months ago, when it suddenly turned aggressive.'

'What do you suggest?' said Lady Werth. 'That something has happened in this past year to rile the Books?'

'I hardly know,' said Gussie. 'But it is an idea worth the considering, is it not?'

'But what could it have been?' said Lady Werth. 'There was no contact between the two Books until the second was brought here. How could anything have affected them both, and at the same time?'

'I do not know, Aunt, and perhaps I am quite wrong. But I mean to bear the notion in mind, for we do not know it to be impossible, either. Do we?'

Lord and Lady Werth exchanged a worried look. 'I believe I will write again to my acquaintance,' said Lady Werth. 'You are perfectly right, Gussie. If there are more such Books in the world, it may prove imperative to learn of them.'

The conclave continued for some time, though without producing any more information Gussie considered relevant. The conversation passed on from the subject of the Book, nobody having anything further to say upon the subject. She herself lingered only long enough to hold some stunted dialogue with her vanished parents, by way of Nell as interpreter. The experience proved an uncomfortable one, for she was obliged to address the empty air; replies reached her through Nell's lips.

And she had no notion what to say to them. What remarks *did* one address to the parents one had never met, after all? She could hardly enquire after their health, and little about her own life seemed worthy of report. Unlike Nell, she had no husband to speak of with winning fondness, nor children whose exploits might be companionably laughed over. She stayed in the room out of politeness only, and excused herself as soon as she could.

'Nell will manage very well without us,' she said to Miss Frostell, as they walked slowly back in the direction of Gussie's cottage.

'Do not you think she was looking rather tired?'

'I did,' Gussie owned. 'The conclave always is exhausting, I believe. But she will retire directly to bed once it is finished, and she need not leave it again until she is recovered. She will be very well again by tomorrow, I am sure.'

'What a pity it is that Mr. Thannibour did not come with her, or the dear children. They would have been so charmingly reviving for her.'

'No such thing. Arthur, perhaps, might be; but the children could only have plagued her to death. Far better for her to recover in peace, and return to the bosom of her family in a day or two.'

The two ladies proceeded as far as the shrubbery without either venturing another remark. There, however, they encountered Lord Bedgberry, striding in from somewhere across the park. The hem of his dark great-coat swirled around his ankles, his hat shadowed his eyes, and his face was reddened with the cold.

'You have missed all the excitement, I'm afraid,' said Gussie, pausing in the middle of the path. 'Though if you want to say anything to the deceased, there may still be time.'

'I can't think what,' said Theo.

'No, nor could I. We did not find out a great deal about the Book, either, though one point stands confirmed: it *has* killed at least one of us, in the past.'

'Bertha?'

'Yes. Though she did not herself appear, so we do not know how it came about.'

'I am more concerned with the question of why,' said Theo. 'Why should it attack some of us, but not others? Why is it sometimes quiescent, and at other times murderous? There isn't a particle of sense about any of it.'

'I do not see why you should expect consistency of behaviour from a Book. After all, *you* are sometimes harmless enough, and at other times perfectly brutal.'

'Yes, but I am not a collection of pages bound in leather.'

'What has that to say to anything?'

'One *expects* consistency of behaviour from books. Their purpose in existing could hardly be clearer.'

'You are speaking of the inanimate kind. It isn't at all the same.'

'So I am.'

'Everyone is gathered in my aunt's parlour, if you want to catch the end of the conclave.'

Theo nodded, and passed into the house.

'For my part, I am tired of the subject,' said Gussie, as she and Miss Frostell paced on. 'The nasty thing may rot in the cellar for the rest of the day; I shan't waste another thought on it.'

This she knew to be a lie, and so it proved, for her thoughts circled uselessly around the problem for the rest of the afternoon. By the time she and Miss Frostell retired to bed, she had produced half of another piece of fancy-work. She had begun with the intention of embroidering something innocuous and cheering, like a glade of flowers, but what she produced was yet another representation of the Book. Flames curled hungrily around its covers, and half of its pages were already burned away.

FIVE

The next event of note consisted of a reply, by letter, from Lady Maundevyle. This missive, penned upon the very best hot-pressed paper, and smelling faintly of something floral, was delivered to Gussie's cottage late upon the following morning, and brought to her by her maid.

'From the Towers, miss,' said the maid, putting the paper, seal broken, into Gussie's hands. 'Her ladyship had it sent over.'

Gussie quickly opened it up.

'What an unconscionable scrawl,' she said, much struck by the poor quality of the handwriting. 'Her last letter was not near so bad.'

'What does it say?' said Miss Frostell, looking up from her labours. She was engaged in stitching Gussie's latest creative masterpiece into matched panels of burgundy brocade, and stuffing them with cotton.

'She declines our invitation.'

'Oh!' Miss Frostell dropped her needle.

'Yes, but it isn't so bad as all that. Listen: "I find myself unequal to travel at this season, but it would afford me the greatest pleasure to see you, Georgiana. We were the best of friends in our youth, were not we? If you should find it possible to venture through such uninviting weather, you will find a warm welcome awaiting you, and all your dear family, at Starminster. Our Christmas celebrations are, I believe, second to none." There is more, but that is the gist of it.' Gussie folded up the letter, and sat in thought.

'You are not pleased at the prospect, my dear?' said Miss Frostell, uncertain how to interpret this silence.

'I am wondering at it. Lady Maundevyle is not a guileless woman. I am persuaded she does nothing without a clear motive. What can be her intentions in proposing to carry all of us off to Starminster?'

'It may be that she is sincere in what she's said,' ventured Miss Frostell. 'I myself deplore travelling in the winter. It is so uncomfortable.'

'Maybe that's it,' Gussie allowed. She read the letter through again, eager for some clue as to what may be afoot at Starminster. But the letter was opaque. She had not even made any reference to her eldest son's protracted stay at Werth Towers, and while she had extended her invitation to include Lady Werth's family, she had made no personal mention of Gussie. That it could not be a mere social invitation, Gussie was fully persuaded. But what Lady Maundevyle might intend by it, she could make no guess whatsoever.

'Well,' she said cheerfully, setting the letter aside. 'We shall proceed as we did in the summer, of course. The only way to find out what she wants is to go there, though ideally we shall be permitted the use of our own carriage this time. Shall you come with us, Frosty? You will not mind the discomfort of the journey, if there are to be festivities.'

'Her ladyship spoke of your family, my dear.'

'And are you not a part of it?'

Miss Frostell, pink with pleasure, bent over her stitching. 'I own, I should prefer not to be alone at the Towers for Christmas.'

'I am certain my aunt and uncle can have no objection.'

Nor did they, though by the time Gussie had completed the more difficult task of persuading them to go themselves, her request to add Miss Frostell to the party came as a mere triviality.

'I do so hate to be away from the Towers at Christmas,' sighed Lady Werth. 'And to spend it in so inhospitable an environment, too!'

'Starminster is nothing of the sort,' Gussie assured her. 'Our hostess may be somewhat lacking, but her house and her servants are anything but. We will be very comfortable.'

'I believe I will leave you to tell Theo,' said Lady Werth, with the nearest thing to ill-nature as she could manage to muster towards her niece. 'He will dislike the notion excessively.'

Gussie accepted this duty without question. After all, it *was* all her fault. 'Yes, but that did not prevent him from going there before,' she pointed out.

Lady Werth proved correct, however. Theo took violent exception to the prospect.

'No!' he snapped. 'Nothing could induce me!'

'But Theo—'

'No. I shall remain here. Someone must keep a watch over the Books, or had you not thought of that?'

'The servants are—'

'Ill-equipped to manage them, as you well know.'

She had been so unwise as to venture up to the east tower for the purposes of importuning him. Irritation with the intrusion made him speak hastily, she was sure.

But he remained unmoved.

Though she would never own it, Gussie could not altogether blame him.

Nell's visit to the Towers was not a protracted one. She never would consent to be parted from her family for very long together, which was almost enough to bring Gussie around to Miss Frostell's way of thinking.

She broached the subject on the morning of Nell's departure, having secured some portion of her sister's time to herself. Nell arrived at the cottage laden with assorted articles of interest: two books from her uncle's library, intended for Arthur's use; a Paisley shawl Gussie recognised as formerly belonging to her aunt; and a set of shoe-roses in Gussie's favourite rose-pink hue. These last she presented to Gussie herself, with rather a distracted air, laying the rest of her burdens upon the parlour sofa. 'I saw these at the haberdasher's and had to buy them for you,' she said. 'And then, with one thing or another, they quite went out of my head until this morning.'

'They are perfect,' Gussie said, smiling in delight, and kissed her sister's cheek in gratitude. 'How kind of you to think of me. And what with Christmas at Starminster, I may even have an opportunity to wear them!'

'At Starminster?' Nell sank onto the sofa next to her books and shawl, looking quizzically at Gussie. 'Whatever for?'

She still appeared wearied, Gussie thought, though she wore it well. The consequences of parenthood, perhaps. 'We are invited,' she said. 'And my aunt and uncle have consented to go.'

'Most unusual, is not it?'

'Yes, but we are only going so that we may ransack the place in search of violently aggressive Books, or anything pertaining to them. His lordship does have an excellent library.'

'Surely a letter to Lord Maundevyle would achieve the same purpose?'

'It might, but his lordship is not at home. In fact, I haven't a notion where he is.'

Nell, whose attention had wandered to the tea-tray set out upon a low table, looked sharply at her sister. 'Was not he here, haunting my aunt's shrubbery?'

'He was.'

'And?'

'And I may have dispatched him upon an errand which, I collect, is proving difficult to carry out.'

'In the dead of winter? Gussie!'

'Before you say any more, you must know that Theo had the same idea. He would have asked the thing of his lordship, if I had not.'

'Oh, then your conduct is entirely beyond reproach.'

'Of course it is.'

'Her ladyship, then? Is not she still at Starminster?'

'Yes, but one can hardly rely upon her to follow even the simplest of instructions. Besides, I must go myself so that I can find out what happens if I shake hands with her.'

'You think she will turn dragon, like her son?'

'Or lycanthrope, like her other son. I couldn't say what her Wyrde may prove to be, and I could not say that I care. It is my own Wyrde that interests me.'

Finding this perfectly reasonable, Nell nodded. 'Write to me, and tell me everything that happens. I shall be living in suspense until you do.'

Gussie took a seat next to her sister, carefully moving the paraphernalia from the Towers out of the way. 'In point of fact, I was hoping you might consent to go with us.'

'But Arthur, and the children—'

'May come along, too. Her ladyship's invitation was extended to *all* Aunt Werth's "dear family", after all.'

Nell sighed. 'And I should love to spend Christmas with you all, but not at Starminster. Gussie, you said yourself that those Selwyns are deranged. And the last time you were there, half of the house came down.'

'You do not think the children would be safe.'

'Could you promise it?'

Gussie could guarantee nothing of the kind, and she did not make the attempt. 'After Christmas, then?' she tried. 'Bring everyone to the Towers. My aunt and uncle would love it if you did.'

'But the Books,' said Nell. 'I am not persuaded the children would be safe here, either. But, Gussie, *you* may visit us, may not you? Allow me to extend an invitation, on Arthur's behalf as well as my own. I know he would love to see you.'

Gussie, together with her aunt, had been to Fothingale Manor only once. The visit had taken place soon after Nell's marriage to Arthur Thannibour, and while brief, it had been a source of great happiness to Gussie. But the first of Nell's children had been born soon afterwards, and with the succession of young Thannibours that had since followed, there had been no opportunity for repeating the visit.

'I would be delighted to come,' Gussie said, clasping her sister's hand. 'If I shall not be terribly in the way.' She made a show of examining Nell's figure, neatly confined as it was in a plain woollen gown of slate-blue. 'You won't be presenting poor Arthur with any more hopeful offspring before the spring, I trust?'

Nell blushed, and laughed. 'I trust *not*. Neither before the spring, nor after it, if I had my way.'

'Four children must be enough for anyone,' Gussie agreed.

'Gussie, I cannot be easy about poor Lord Maundevyle. Has he been gone for the whole winter?'

Gussie, having never given the matter the least thought, was obliged to stop a moment before making any reply. 'It was not so very cold yet, when he left,' she decided. 'I believe it was not yet the end of October.'

'Then he has been gone these six weeks at least,' said Nell.

'Why, so he has. I had no notion that it had been so long.'

'Gus, what did you ask him to do?'

'*We*, that being Theo and I, entreated him to bring Lady Margery back to the Towers.'

'Not on account of those terrible Books?' said Nell.

'Again?'

'Yes, of course it is about the Books. And it was a much better notion than having Felix hold that dreadful ritual again, was it not?'

'Assuming Lord Maundevyle does not perish of the cold,' said Nell.

Gussie gave her sister's hand an impulsive squeeze. 'I am almost inclined to wish that I could care about people as you do, Nell, only I am persuaded it must be very uncomfortable. Look, you are got quite into a lather of worry, and I am sure there isn't the least need.'

'How should you like to be away from home for six weeks in the winter, and with nowhere to sleep?'

'Now, what should give you the idea that he hasn't anywhere to sleep? He is a grown man, Nell, and can shift for himself very well.'

'I suppose you are right.'

'And then, he is a dragon. I am not perfectly certain of it, but I should be surprised if he was much affected by the cold.'

Nell rose to her feet, and collected up her acquisitions. 'No, I am sure you are right,' she said. 'And I must put the matter from my mind, for it is time I departed. My carriage will have been ready this half-hour at least.'

Gussie parted with her sister reluctantly, as she always did. If there was one person in the world whom she could say she fervently missed, it would be Nell.

'Come to me in the spring,' Nell repeated, bending to kiss Gussie's cheek. 'We will be looking forward to it with *very* great pleasure.'

'I'll come,' Gussie promised. 'If I possibly can.'

Nell's departure left Gussie feeling bereft, and a little disappointed with the world. With too little to occupy her, she was in danger of descending into the glooms, were it not for Miss Frostell. That good lady jollied Gussie's spirits at every opportunity; held herself ready at any moment for a walk across the park (weather permitting), or tea at the Towers; and engaged in many a tête-à-tête over the tea-table. She shamelessly encouraged the very worst excesses of Gussie's fancy-work, and by the end of another two weeks, the neat, snug rooms at Lake Cottage each bore a collection of highly original cushions. One developed the additional advantage of a silk screen painted up with a jumble of images, chief amongst these being the crimson-scaled form of a dragon curled up along the bottom.

By such means did Gussie contrive to pass the slow December days, until at last the appointed day for their departure to Starminster approached. Wishing, once again, for Nell, she packed her shoe-roses; made a final, useless attempt to persuade Theo into joining the party; parried all of Great-Aunt Honoria's wicked raillery upon the subject of the absent Lord Maundevyle; and spent no inconsiderable time soothing Lady Werth's qualms about the visit.

'I shall be ice from head to toe inside of an hour, I am sure of it,' said she, checking her portmanteau yet again for any useful articles she may have forgotten. 'Or Lady Maundevyle will.'

'Be easy, Aunt,' said Gussie. 'I have ensured that you have everything you could possibly need; nothing is forgotten. And you will be too warm and merry to ice anybody.'

'But what if she is to become anything very bad? You have not the smallest idea what will become of your Wyrding her, now do you?'

'If she does, then you may ice her with everybody's blessing.' Gussie added, as a happy thought occurred to her, 'You may ice Clarissa right away, if you should feel disposed. Doing so can only improve the visit.'

'She cannot be as bad as all that.'

'Cannot she? Do please recollect that she kidnapped me last summer, and wearing men's dress besides.'

Lady Werth raised her eyebrows at her niece. 'Which is

not at all the sort of escapade you would get into yourself.'

'I should never dream of such impropriety.'

'I believe you are sorry you did not think of it first.'

'Nonsense,' said Gussie roundly, and without a particle of truth.

'I do wish Lord Maundevyle had come back,' said Lady Werth. 'If he should return over Christmas, and perhaps with Lady Margery, they will find no one to welcome them but Theo.'

Gussie did not waste any time assuring her aunt that Lord Bedgberry would manage the business very well. 'Lord Maundevyle, at least, is used to Theo,' she said. 'In fact, it's my belief they have even become friends.'

'Unaccountable.'

'Isn't it? As for Lady Margery, provided she is well fed it does not seem likely that she will much object to a little peace and quiet.'

The party for Starminster, once assembled in Lord Werth's heavy travelling coach, consisted of five altogether. Lord and Lady Werth, Gussie herself, and Miss Frostell occupied the seats, and Great-Aunt Honoria's head floated an inch or so beneath the ceiling.

Gussie let down the window, and sat with her head poking out of it, surveying the great doors of the Towers and the empty drive-way beyond. 'I'm afraid he is not coming out, Aunt.'

Lady Werth, tight-lipped and fretful, made no response.

'It is of no moment,' said Lord Werth. 'Theo will be perfectly well, my dear, and we do not need him to see us off.'

Privately, Gussie imagined it probable that her cousin had forgotten his bosom family's imminent departure. 'Probably he is engaged with the Books,' she said gravely. 'But do not let that alarm you, Aunt. He will have his axe with him, and therefore I don't at all suppose we shall return to find him torn to pieces.'

Lord Werth responded to this sally with a quelling look, and thumped the coach's ceiling thrice in the signal to drive on. 'Be easy, my love,' he said to his wife. 'Consider how very quiet we have all been these past several weeks. Nothing untoward is the least likely to happen before we return.'

'If that were *all* I had to occupy me,' said Lady Werth, as the coach lurched into motion, 'I should be easy indeed.'

'Aye,' said Great-Aunt Honoria, her head swivelling to look out of the window. 'We shall be doing very well if *we* do not turn up dismembered before our return.'

'It does not appear to have done *you* any very great harm,' Gussie observed.

Honoria gave a cackle. 'Very right, my dear! Oh, but we are forgetting Silvester!' This reflection horrified her, for she attempted a low dive out of the window Gussie had yet to fully close.

Gussie caught at her hair. 'Pray be composed, Aunt. Silvester remains in support of Theo.' Or at least, that is what she hoped he had said. His rambling comments had covered a great deal of ground, from the merits of a good ragout to the finer points of some prize mare he had once owned, and which must by now be long since rotted. Since he had not presented himself at the coach, and was not to be discerned clinging to any part of its frame, Gussie chose to believe he had heard her plea, and elected to remain with Theo.

For, while she possessed not a tenth of the concern poor Lady Werth suffered under, she was not wholly free of it either. All things considered, they would both of them have felt easier had Theo consented to come along.

SIX

The Starminster estate had lost none of its splendour since Gussie's last visit, despite Lord Maundevyle's unfortunate encounter with the roof. If anything, it had grown even grander.

'I am almost positive it was not this big before,' said Gussie, head once more stuck out of the open window, as the Werth travelling coach drew up to the mansion house. 'Can a building embiggen itself?'

'Embiggen?' said Lady Werth, as yet unenlightened by a glimpse of the Maundevyle home.

'Enlargen,' Gussie allowed.

'I am not sure that is a word either.'

Great-Aunt Honoria, too impatient to await the stopping of the coach or the opening of the doors, drifted upwards, and passed through the roof. 'It *is* larger!' she called. 'I could almost swear to it.'

'A building may be enlarged,' said Lord Werth. 'By architects and workmen, via the use of suitable materials and tools. But as to whether or not a house may simply grow bigger, as I understand you to mean, then I should think not.'

'Coming from the mouth of the most Werthish of

Patriarchs, that is a statement to carry some weight,' said Gussie. 'After all, what Lord Werth does not know about the peculiar can hardly be worth talking of.'

'Werthish?' said Lady Werth. The doors being that moment opened by a pair of uniformed footmen, she got down directly, and stood looking up at the Starminster mansion in momentary awe. 'I see what you mean,' she said.

'Werth Towers is nothing to it,' said Gussie cheerfully, following her aunt onto the drive-way.

'Not half!' carolled Lady Honoria.

'I beg you will not let Lady Maundevyle hear you say that,' said Lady Werth, venturing up to the tall, double doors. 'Or we shall never hear the end of it.'

'Nothing could persuade me to own the slightest inferiority to the Selwyns,' Gussie assured her. 'Not on any point whatsoever.'

Lady Maundevyle herself was discovered to be standing in the centre of her grandiose hall, patently waiting for them. Whether she had stationed some hapless minion to watch for their approach, with orders to fetch her immediately, or whether she had amused herself by standing there all the morning in anticipation of their arrival, Gussie did not like to guess. It appeared to her all too possible that the witless woman might have chosen the latter course.

'Welcome!' said she in ringing tones, spreading her arms wide. She had clearly prepared with great care for her guests' arrival, for her attire was sumptuous almost to the point of absurdity. She wore a gown of pure, wine-coloured silk, heavily embroidered; the shawl slung elegantly over her elbows was the finest froth of lace; and her *jewels*! Gussie thanked her stars that the summer was past, and the strong sunshine with it, or the quantity of diamonds the Dowager Viscountess thought fit to wear must have blinded them all. She even wore a few in her handsomely coiffed hair.

Gussie felt quite the dowd in the simple, forest-green travelling dress she wore, but impatiently suppressed the feeling. The display was evidently calculated to produce exactly that effect, and had she not refused to consider herself the slightest bit inferior to the Selwyns?

Her aunt and uncle comported themselves with the utmost dignity as they made their greetings to their hostess, and Gussie copied their example as she made her own curtsey. The Werths' public manners might be a shade old-fashioned, but her aunt and uncle could never be faulted for courtesy. Not, at least, as long as they were tolerably comfortable.

Theo was another matter.

'Has dear Lord Bedgberry not accompanied you?' asked Lady Maundevyle, once the introductions and pleasantries were over.

'My son finds himself detained by urgent business at the Towers,' said Lady Werth.

'A great pity. My younger son has also pleaded some urgent errand, but we mothers would never like to think they are avoiding these pleasant family gatherings?'

'The thought would never have entered my head,' said Lady Werth.

'But Miss Werth will be delighted to meet Clarissa again, and perhaps Henry as well. I have ordered the best of rooms to be made available for you; no doubt you would wish to rest after your journey—'

'Henry?' interrupted Gussie, perceiving that neither her aunt nor her uncle would be so rude as to do so. 'Surely you cannot mean that he is here?'

'Why, yes,' said her ladyship, with a smile Gussie would term *silky*. 'Had you not expected to find him here, in his own home, at Christmas?'

For once in her life, Gussie was bereft of speech.

'Delightful,' interposed Lady Werth smoothly. 'We shall take great pleasure in seeing Lord Maundevyle again. But first, I for one would be pleased to accept your kind invitation of a rest before dinner.'

Lady Maundevyle bowed her head. 'Miss Werth will find her former suite of rooms given over to her use, and I have ordered the Dragon Suite prepared for you. I trust you will be pleased with it.'

'A new addition, I fancy?' Gussie guessed.

'You will find a number of changes about the place since your last visit, Miss Werth. Our family's return to the Wyrde is worthy of celebration, is it not?'

'By redecorating in reflection of your elder son's Wyrde? How original,' said Lady Werth.

'How strange that we should never have hit upon so happy a notion ourselves,' added Gussie.

Gussie had previously gone away with the melancholy suspicion that the dowager was impervious to irony. So it again proved. Her smile held no trace of chagrin; her eyes brightened with pleasure. 'The Selwyns have ever been a source of inspiration to the world,' said she.

Gussie, having enjoyed enough of the dowager's society for the present, declared herself exhausted. 'I'll just go up to my rooms, if I may,' said she, anxious to escape before Miss Selwyn could join them. 'I believe I can remember the way.'

'Miss Frostell,' said the dowager, before Gussie could get away. 'You are not yourself Wyrded, I believe?'

How impertinent a question! Gussie bristled; but Miss Frostell, incapable of resentment, merely said: 'Not in the least, your ladyship.'

'Very well. Then you will be comfortable in the Yellow Room.'

Miss Frostell made her bow.

'Please,' said Lady Maundevyle, her smile embracing the whole family. 'While you are here, I trust you will treat Starminster as though it were your own home. Lord Werth, you will find me ready to conduct you out to the family plot at any time you name. It is nothing to compare to your charming churchyard at the Towers, I dare say, but you will not find it wholly contemptible. My ancestors' graves are at your complete disposal.'

Lord Werth must have been stupefied with delight, for he found nothing to say.

'As for my dear Georgiana, should you wish to practice your own, estimable arts, you will find my servants quite ready to oblige you. I have taken the liberty of securing some additional help for the season. You may, therefore, disport yourself at your leisure, without the smallest fear of inconveniencing the household.'

Gussie, perceiving her aunt's face darkening with anger, hastily stepped in. 'How obliging, ma'am. May I hope that you have also provided for Lady Honoria? My Great-Aunt requires very little in the way of sustenance; only an occasional taste of gibbering terror, no more.'

'Oh, but it is the season for merrymaking!' sang Honoria, with a vicious smile. 'You would not have me suffer such scant rations over Christmas, Gussie dear?'

'Quite right, Aunt. I had forgotten that.'

'My servants—' began Lady Maundevyle.

'Oh, no,' purred Great-Aunt Honoria, descending from her lofty position to look her ladyship in the eye. 'Truly superior terror requires a superior personage, does not it?'

'Without question,' said Gussie.

'A maid may take fright at anything; I have known it to happen over the most trivial of things. But the terror of a viscountess! Only think how delightful!'

'Ah, but,' said Gussie, 'We are in the presence of only a *dowager* viscountess, Aunt.'

'We all make do,' sighed Honoria. 'When we must.'

Their hostess, betraying her irritation by a tightening about the mouth, returned to what Gussie recognised as her rehearsed speech. 'Miss Werth,' she said, 'will not be surprised to learn that I am eager to hold conversation with her.'

'I suppose I shan't, but you need not importune me immediately?' said Gussie. 'I cannot guarantee tolerable results unless I have had a rest first. Why, the last person to turn Wyrded in my presence became a gorgon, and I *was* feeling rather harried that morning. You would not like a head full of snakes, ma'am, I think?'

'You are forgetting my sons,' said Lady Maundevyle. 'The Selwyn Wyrde is never contemptible.'

'You would like to turn dragon, would you? I might have guessed,' sighed Gussie. 'In that case, ma'am, I shall be obliged to you if you would satisfy a few, trifling demands? Scarcely anything to regard, I assure you, but since they will please me greatly, they are sure to be productive of excellent results.'

'My house and my servants are yours to command, Miss Werth.'

Gussie's eyes brightened. 'Marvellous. Then I would like a suite of rooms for Miss Frostell, please, preferably adjacent to my own.'

'Of course,' said the dowager, with a slight inclination of her head. If the words were uttered through gritted teeth, she hid the fact well.

Gussie thought. 'An array of pastries for breakfast every morning, to be delivered to my rooms. I do feel so much livelier if I am suitably supplied with confectionery.' Gussie had no qualms *here*; if the wretched woman had indeed hired extra help over Christmas, in the absurd belief that Lady Werth would amuse herself by icing half of them, then a daily selection of cakes should prove but a small charge upon the kitchen.

'If you will be so good as to furnish me with a list of your favourites, it shall be attended to,' promised Lady Maundevyle.

'Wonderful,' Gussie smiled, warming to her theme. 'Now, my uncle may like to raise corpses at any moment, you know. He once left a dinner halfway through, though the guests numbered among them a duke! Perhaps a footman assigned to his personal use, ready to conduct him out to the family graves at a moment's notice?'

'There will not be the smallest difficulty,' said the dowager, tightly smiling.

'He had better have a strong stomach, poor man. Few can bear the sight of the decomposed human form without suffering a spasm.'

'I am sure it has caused *you* many a trying hour,' said Lady Maundevyle.

But this paltry attempt at malice fell short, for Gussie said without turning a hair, 'No, not a one. But I was a thorough Werth from birth, you know, and received early training.'

The dowager viscountess's smile faltered.

'Poor Nurse Scot *would* be jealous of the new nanny. Nothing could persuade her to give way, though she had been dead several years.'

'So trying,' sighed Lady Werth. 'I believe we went through half a dozen a year.'

'Corpses?' said Lady Maundevyle, one brow raised.

'Nannies,' said Lady Werth.

'Both,' said Lord Werth.

Perhaps it was pitiful to take satisfaction in having disconcerted the dowager, but Gussie smiled. 'I believe that will do for the present, ma'am. And now for that rest I mentioned?'

'For shame,' said Lady Werth somewhat later, having ventured to visit her niece in her own suite of rooms. 'A list of demands! Gussie, I was quite ashamed.'

'Oh, but why?' said Gussie, maliciously smiling. 'If I must be put to use, like a cart horse, or a footman, then why should not we get the most out of it? And it is shameful of her to put poor Frosty in some paltry Yellow Room, as though she were not every bit as important as I am.'

'But you cannot in the smallest degree alter her Wyrde, can you? So that was a shameless untruth.'

'Yes, it was.'

Her long-suffering aunt sighed.

'Though to be perfectly truthful, I am not *certain* that it was, and neither are you. We yet require further information. Who knows but what I might make dragons of the lot of us, if I chose?'

'Perhaps you might practice upon the servants,' said Lady Werth acidly. 'Esther having been so plentiful with them, I am sure there will be enough to go round.'

'I struggle to picture the two of you ever having been friends,' said Gussie. 'Esther! The dowager has a name, just as though she, too, were a regular person.'

'She was not so strange, when we were young. Or, I do not recollect that she was. The years altered her.'

'Perhaps she was simply better at hiding it, once,' said Gussie. 'I refuse to believe she was ever anything other than monstrously deranged.'

'I fear you may be right. Have you yet seen Lord Maundevyle? I hardly know how to account for his being *here*, when we expected him at the Towers.'

'With Lady Margery in tow,' said Gussie. 'I am disappointed, I own. But at least he need no longer be worried over. While *you*, my dear aunt, were picturing him frozen to death in pursuit of our wayward ancestress, he must have been enjoying every comfort at home.'

'I cannot think why he would not have sent word, at least,' said Lady Werth.

Gussie, refreshed from an hour's repose, and as delighted with her rose-coloured rooms as before, collected her ivory woollen shawl in a happy humour. 'Let us go and find him, then, and see what we may find out.'

'He is in the library,' said Great-Aunt Honoria, her head erupting through the wall. 'I saw him there not two minutes ago. He is reading a book!'

'Shocking conduct,' murmured Gussie.

'Sitting at his ease, as though he had not sent our entire family out of our heads with worry over him!'

'Not the *entire* family, Aunt,' said Gussie.

'True, there is no discombobulating Theo,' Honoria

allowed.

'I was thinking of myself. Theo was moved enough to spare at least a thought or two for his lordship's possible fate.'

Great-Aunt Honoria's mouth stretched wide in a horrific grin. 'But you are made of sterner stuff, are not you?' she said, and vanished.

'In one or two particulars,' Gussie agreed.

Gussie had, to the last, been prepared for some odd twist to emerge; the true Lord Maundevyle proving to be nowhere near Starminster, as expected, and his mother a liar. But indeed, there he was. Reclining by an exquisite marble hearth, within which roared a comfortable blaze; dressed in his dark blue coat and pale waistcoat, and looking the very height of elegance; glancing up as the three ladies entered, with the smile of a man perfectly at ease.

'Lady Werth, Miss Werth,' said he. 'Lady Honoria. Just the pleasure I was hoping for.'

'We were rather hoping for the pleasure of *your* company, too,' Gussie said.

'But not *here*,' added Lady Honoria, a vision of displeasure. She swooped into his lordship's face, and bared what was left of her teeth. 'What a dance you've led us!'

'Peace, Honoria,' said Lady Werth.

'We ought not to take issue with his lordship for sitting cosily by his own hearth,' Gussie agreed. 'Where else has he a better right to sit?'

Henry, Lord Maundevyle, inspected his audience in momentary silence, and set aside his book. 'I perceive I am in disgrace. But you may be a little softened if you will permit me to explain.'

'Nothing would delight us more,' Gussie assured him.

He was observed to smile, very slightly, if one happened to be paying close attention. 'I found Lady Margery,' he began.

Gussie suspected him of a mischievous desire to disarm criticism, perhaps at his audience's expense. The traces of a smile deepened, especially when Lady Honoria, overpowered with enthusiasm, shot clear up to the ceiling.

'You did!' said Lady Werth. 'I had not imagined it an errand likely to succeed, I confess.'

'Nor was it,' said Lord Maundevyle. 'I was obliged to visit near every refectory of note across three counties before I found traces of her.'

'Refectories?' Gussie demanded. 'Is that what you've been doing all this time? Dining?'

The smile widened; it was joined by a deeply appreciative chuckle.

'You've waited weeks to see the look on my face when you said that, haven't you?' said Gussie.

'It was worth every moment of suspense.'

Gussie, remembering Lady Margery's delight in a sophisticated meal, thought his lordship's method bordering upon genius. But it would never do to admit as much. 'I like that!' said she, setting her hands upon her hips. 'My poor aunts all in a twitter over your probable demise, and you gorging on sides of beef all this while.'

'And venison,' said Lord Maundevyle. 'Some particularly excellent roast pork, at the Red Lion coaching-inn near Ipswich. Perfect raised pies, stuffed with every good thing, and pastries of the utmost delicacy—'

'I should leave off, if I were you,' Gussie recommended. 'A joke ought never to be belaboured, however good in itself, and I perceive that one or another of my aunts shall soon be tempted to do you an injury.'

Lord Maundevyle subsided. 'I found Lady Margery in Bath,' he said. 'Causing a stir in the pump-rooms, as you may imagine.'

'Bath!' said Lady Werth. 'I never heard that there was anything good to be eaten *there.*'

'Evidently she agreed, for she was in a rare temper when I ran her to earth. Seeing as Bath is a deal nearer to

Starminster than to the Towers, I brought her here by the simple means of offering her a superior repast. I believe she's presently to be found outside the Orangery, partaking of a veal pie, a grilled salmon, and a haunch of boar, with salmagundy and stewed potatoes, and a Floating Island pudding.'

Gussie, fascinated, attempted to picture this vision of gluttony. 'I shouldn't think even so magnificent a dinner would be near enough to satisfy a dragon-sized appetite.'

'Except that they are dragon-sized portions. It has taken the kitchens a full day to prepare it all. You find me recovering from the rare exertion of penning a letter, addressed to you, which I suppose I may now burn. Since I understood from my mother that you were to come here, I did not think it worth the effort of returning to the Towers.'

Gussie smiled. 'How disappointing. We must put away our indignation, and muster some gratitude in its place.'

'Indignation is always the more entertaining of the two,' Lord Maundevyle agreed. 'It comes with so agreeable a sensation of outrage.'

'Which adds wonderfully to one's consequence. Has Lady Margery said anything much to the purpose?'

'About the Books, I collect you mean? Not yet. She declared herself half starved, equal to nothing until she had dined suitably.'

'Then I hope your cook is an artist in the kitchen,' Gussie said, making for the door. 'If you do not mind, I believe I will brave the cold and go in search of her immediately. If we should feel the need to resign your mother's hospitality early—'

'Which you think probable,' interjected Lord Maundevyle.

'—then I would like to have talked with her already, and yes, I think it extremely probable.'

Lady Margery's splendid bulk lay sprawled in emerald-glimmering splendour across the remains of a grand ornamental garden. The head gardener's pride and joy lay crushed, the intricate patterns of neatly-trimmed hedges ruined. Lady Maundevyle might think herself fortunate that the delicate panes of frosted glass making up the Orangery itself had escaped harm.

Stretched out in a posture of blissful repletion, wings folded and snout fixed in a dreamy smile, Lady Margery was a vision of happy hedonism. Gussie espied a litter of bones and enormous platters abandoned here and there, plus the wary faces of a small army of servants, poised either to serve the dragon or take away the wreckage as required.

'I wonder that your mother did not mention Margery's presence,' said Gussie. 'I could almost suspect her of deliberate subterfuge, except that I am sure she must be delighted by the presence of another dragon.'

'I asked her not to,' admitted Lord Maundevyle, taking stock of the damage with a philosophical air. 'I wanted to surprise you.'

'It was a good joke,' Gussie allowed.

He looked sideways at her. 'I asked myself what Miss Werth might have done in the circumstances, and soon hit upon the happy notion of lying to you.'

'I am delighted to be a source of inspiration to the world, as your dear mama might put it.'

'I hope I did it well,' he pursued.

'You are eager for a compliment.'

'I have worked hard for one, you must allow.'

Thinking of the weeks his lordship had spent searching through all the best public eating-houses across three counties, Gussie would not deny it. 'We are most grateful to you,' she said. 'Truly.'

'I believe you almost to be sincere,' he said, in a marvelling tone.

She smiled. 'About *that* I am sincere indeed. If I congratulate you likewise for your burgeoning skill at dissembling, shall you suspect me of a polite falsehood?'

'No. In *that* I believe you to speak nothing but truth.'

Walking around Lady Margery's grand bulk in pursuit of a conversation, Gussie's view of the scene enlarged. The dragon lay with eyes closed, snout resting atop her folded feet. Upon reaching that great face, Gussie beheld her great-aunt, attempting to wake the sleeping beast by dint of bawling insults into the nearest of her ears; and Clarissa Selwyn, helping herself to the remains lurking at the bottom of a wood-carved bowl the size of a cart wheel.

'I always was partial to Floating Island pudding,' said Miss Selwyn. She was seated in a cross-legged position upon the chipped stones, an indecorous posture rendered possible by the men's garb she once again wore. For some reason, she had adopted a shabby example of the three-corner hats popular in the previous century, an accessory now confined to old men clinging to the fashions of their youth. 'It was papa's,' said she, noticing the direction of Gussie's gaze. 'A favourite with him, so I think it quite heartless of mama to throw it out. Henry rescued it for me.' She held the bowl out to Gussie. 'There is a bit of custard left.'

'Crème anglaise,' snapped Lady Margery without opening her eyes.

Miss Selwyn was unmoved. 'It is the same thing.'

'But "custard" is so common,' said Gussie. 'The correct term carries with it all the cachet of the Parisian artiste.'

'Do not mock gastronomy,' said Lady Margery sternly. 'That is a pursuit for those tragically born without a palate, or any taste.'

Displeased by these reflections upon her commentary, or perhaps in search of more crème anglaise, Miss Selwyn took herself and her bowl away. She favoured Gussie with a parting smile, the confiding kind, which seemed to promise a quantity of girlish intimacies to come. Inwardly, Gussie shuddered.

'I take it you found my cook's efforts to your liking?' said Lord Maundevyle.

The dragon's smile returned; the tip of one sharp incisor protruded. 'I have not hazarded the questionable delights of public eateries in two centuries,' she said. 'And that is because true excellence in cuisine belongs to the private kitchen.'

'Our fashionable watering-places could not satisfy you?' said Great-Aunt Honoria. 'Much to their discredit, I'm sure.'

'Bath is not fashionable nowadays, Aunt,' murmured Gussie. 'Had her ladyship descended upon Brighton, she might have been better pleased.'

'I have better things to do than sojourn at Brighthelmstone,' snorted the dragon. 'A mere, jumped-up nothing of a place.'

'Which nicely disposes of the Prince Regent.'

'The who?'

Lady Werth said, 'The gentleman in whose name parliament now requires the Wyrded among us to register ourselves.'

'*Register*?' gasped the dragon, appalled. 'To what end?'

'Why, to keep track of us, of course,' said Gussie. 'The thing is, some few Wyrded folk have been very badly behaved.'

Margery reared up on her hind legs, her great wings flapping once in indignation. A gust of wind tore at Gussie's gown. 'You mean to tell me,' she fumed, smoke pouring from her nostrils, 'that we are now expected to *behave ourselves*?'

'Like lambs,' Gussie assured her.

'You will have to get a license,' Lady Werth said. 'All the more dangerously Wyrded are to be so obliged, so Mr. Ballantine tells us.'

'A license! To do what?'

'Exist,' said Gussie.

'Well, then,' said Lady Margery, folding up her wings with a *snap*. 'It will be many a long year before I will visit the World again, let me tell you.'

'But before you vanish to distant and unreachable places,' said Gussie, 'pray tell us what you remember about the Book of Werth. It is on *that* subject we wished to consult you, and the matter is becoming pressing.'

'Throttled somebody again, has it?' Lady Margery nodded her huge head.

'Not since Bertha, that we know of,' said Gussie.

'But the thing is becoming so ill-natured,' put in Lady Werth, 'that we are convinced it can only be a matter of time.'

'Not to mention the other one,' said Great-Aunt Honoria.

'The other what?' said the dragon.

'The other Book,' said Gussie, and told the irascible dragon, in as short a speech as possible, all about Mrs. Daventry's curse-book.

'*Those* will certainly have to be licensed,' said Lady Margery with a sneer. 'Not that it will do anyone the smallest good if they were. Why have not you burned them both?'

'Do you think we ought?' said Lady Werth anxiously. 'Only, there is a great deal in the way of family records that will be lost if we do. And I dare not hope the Book will be quiet long enough for them to be copied.'

'I always thought it a foolish scheme, to use the Book for such a purpose,' said Lady Margery. 'Only Ranulf said, "But what use could *we* have for a Bible?", and someone else said — I forget who — "We need only use it for our history. No one would be expected to read the *scripture*." But since there were always a great many of us, a Bible was soon held to be insufficiently capacious, what with so many of the pages being written on already. And so Lord Werth-as-was began writing it all down in the Book, and that was that.' She blew a single, red-tinged plume of smoke from one nostril. 'They ought to have listened to *me*. But it was in one of its tranquil moods at the time, and considered to have got over its tantrums.'

'Where, then, did the Book come from?' said Gussie. 'I had thought it created for the purpose of our family history.'

'No, it was never meant for that. I do not know where it came from. It had always been there.'

'Where exactly?' said Lady Werth.

'The library,' said Lady Margery in surprise. 'Where else?'

'It was not confined?' said Lady Werth.

'Not in my youth. Ranulf would not hear of it.'

'And who was Ranulf?' asked Gussie, bewildered.

'My brother. He had a kindness for the library and all its contents, the fool, and it was of no use to tell him that the thing was not a book.' She smiled toothily. 'He has now been dead these several centuries.'

Great-Aunt Honoria gave an elated gasp. 'You do not mean to say that the *Book* killed him?'

'The matter was never confirmed,' said Lady Margery carelessly. 'But he was discovered throttled, and on the threshold of his beloved book-room.'

'I wonder that you did not burn it then,' said Gussie.

'I never was over fond of Ranulf.'

'You said it was not a book,' said Lady Werth. 'What did you mean by that?'

The dragon's enormous eyes opened wider. 'If you have not observed as much for yourself, you must have a greatly disordered intellect.'

'Patently it has qualities not normally displayed by ordinary library-books,' said Lady Werth. 'But it consists still of a quantity of pages, made out of vellum, and bound between covers—'

'It may have been a book once, but it's my belief that is a mere seeming,' said Lady Margery. 'It is a creature of great cunning.'

'If it is not a book,' said Gussie. 'What is it?'

'If you are very daring, perhaps you may examine it, and find out,' said Lady Margery.

'Theo can do it,' said Gussie at once. 'We may send him a note to that effect, with instructions, and the business might be concluded before ever we arrive home.' In response to the somewhat injured look directed at her by her aunt, she added, 'I am only thinking of the family, Aunt. Sad, helpless souls, most of us, and you would not wish to see us throttled to death?'

'Nor Theo, either?' said Lady Werth.

'Nothing can harm Theo,' said Gussie stoutly. 'And small matter if it did. After all, whatever one may say to the detriment of the world, there will *always* be plenty of Werths.'

SEVEN

The said Theodore Werth, Lord Bedgberry, finding himself alone over Christmas, could hardly believe his luck. He might, for a period of a few blissful weeks, keep his own hours; wander the park from midnight until six, if he chose; sprawl at his leisure in the library otherwise, and help himself to the contents of his father's book-room at will. Nothing could better please him.

Only, with one thing or another, he spent a deal of his time in the cellars.

It began on the day following the departure of the rest of the family, when Theo, reclining at his ease before the library hearth, with a large folio open on his lap and a beverage at his elbow, had got in the way of thinking that he was in for a period of complete enjoyment.

Then came there a whispering, somewhere beyond the door; faint, but persistent.

The servants, of course, talking among themselves. Why they should do so at a whispering volume, he could not have said; dash it, if a man must talk, let him *talk*. But before the noise could disturb him too profoundly, it stopped, and Theo went back to his book.

Only it soon came again, and this time it did not cease after a few minutes. It went on and on, a susurrating, irritating sound, and Theo's attention was wrested entirely from his reading when it occurred to him that he recognised it.

For some moments he sat, rigid with alarm, and could not have moved a muscle even were the library on fire.

The Books.

But no; how could he hear them, all the way in the library? That could not be possible. They were down below, buried deep, suitably smothered.

Unless they were not.

This reflection being enough to propel him straight out of his comfortable chair, he spent a palpitating quarter of an hour in ceaseless activity. But his explorations of the library, the corridor beyond, and the drawing-room adjacent furnished nothing that could explain the sounds. No servants whispering together. No Books (and here he permitted himself a deep sigh of relief), having somehow escaped their prisons, and now upon the rampage.

He met with peace and emptiness everywhere, and he would have been soothed, but that the whispering did not stop.

His steps turned, at length, in the direction of the cold staircase down. Soon he stood in the cellar, ear pressed to the door confining the Book of Werth, listening.

He remained that way for a long time. Half an hour at least, which he judged from the stiff and frozen state of his hands, when he attempted to test the security of the lock. The Books whispered on; until a terrific *crash* came at the door, and the stout oaken boards, sorely tried, threatened to buckle.

Theo, jumping back, and with a ringing in his ears, heard to his horror a dark laugh.

Anger rose, replacing a lurking dread. 'Oh, that is how you propose to treat me, is it?' he snarled, and fetched down the axe (freshly sharpened) which hung by the door-frame. 'I shall be master here one day, and I tell you now: there will be some changes made!' Upon which threat, he unlocked the door, burst into the room, and set about making his feelings known.

A little later, winded and bruised, but exhilarated, he left a subdued Book to think about what it had done, and took himself back upstairs — pausing only to set his ear to the other door, behind which Mrs. Daventry's detestable property languished. He heard nothing from within, and considered himself free to return to his reading.

Ten minutes later the whispering returned.

Enraged, Theo took himself outside, though a light snow fell; and some hours passed before, at great length, he returned to the Towers. The hour was then far advanced, the sun upon the rise, and under *these* conditions, at long last, the cursed Books were silent.

The following sunset found Theo uncharacteristically tense. He positively prowled about the house, hackles raised, his senses alert to every sound and movement. As the wan December light faded away, and the dying sun cast a lurid golden glow over the horizon, Theo stationed himself at the top of the cellar stairs. He did not venture down.

His straining ears detected nothing, not even when the sun died at last, and a dense blackness settled over the Towers.

But the silence felt, to him, palpably malevolent. He stalked back and forth, too restless to settle, for the atmosphere of anticipation, of inevitability, was so thick he could have sliced it quite through with his axe.

The whispering began again.

'Right,' said Theo, hefting the weapon. He inhaled deeply, gathered himself, and roared: '*Great-Uncle Silvesteerrrr!*'

'Bedgberry,' came a gravelly voice, not three feet from his ear.

Excitable as he was, Theo's reflexes betrayed him.

'Well,' he said, admiring, with a guilty eye, the results of his handiwork. 'Not even the Book could get through that.'

The axe-blade being embedded an inch deep in the thick wood of the cellar door, without materially affecting its ability to function, his confidence might be considered reasonable.

Perhaps.

'Nothing like a good fire at Christmas,' said Great-Uncle Silvester. 'Warms the toes nicely. Ring the bell for brandy, Bedgberry.'

'Excellent notion, Uncle.' Theo, whose thoughts had strayed back in the direction of the library, paused. 'Or do you mean a *fire*?'

'The bigger, the better,' Silvester ground out, and then he began to chuckle.

'Do you hear that whispering?'

The chuckling ceased. Theo, whose eyes penetrated the thick darkness in ways he understood to be unusual, beheld the grotesque: perched atop the white-painted frame around the door was he, his stone head tilted. A deeply-graven ear twitched.

'Better put a stop to it,' said Silvester.

'So it isn't just me.' This came as a relief, for Theo had begun to fear he imagined the maddening sounds.

But that meant that it *was* the Books, not merely some temporary derangement of his own wits (or permanent, for that matter). 'They are plotting,' he said. 'Plotting *something* against us.' He sounded paranoid even to his own ears, but he could not help thinking of the long-dead Bertha. 'I would put an end to it in an instant, if I could. But they don't listen.'

'Come and sit by the fire,' recommended Silvester.

'If by that you mean I should burn the things to ash, I'm with you there. Only...' Something caused Theo to hesitate, and it was not the possibility that his mother and father might be displeased to find the family history gone up in smoke. No, it was... it was...

Damn Gussie to hell and back, for it was curiosity he felt. He was *interested!* He wanted badly to know what the Books were saying to one another, and in what arcane and long-forgotten tongue. They *were* books, after all, and what scholar could cheerfully consign them to the flames without first making himself master of everything they had to offer?

It was a conceit worthy of Gussie herself, and how had she contrived to imbue him with this unwelcome aspect of her own personality?

'I want to know,' he growled. 'What they're saying. What they're plotting. I want to know what the Book hides from us, Uncle. Lord Felix was right about that. It hid the ritual; what else has it got in its pages?'

Which put him in mind of his father's promise to raise up the said Lord Felix once again, and interrogate him as to his history with the tome. He hadn't done so. He had fobbed off his family with excuses, then swanned away to Starminster for Christmas without so much as an apology. Yes, Felix was a dead bore, and an extraordinary nuisance, but the man *knew* things.

'Come on,' he said, turning in a trice, and striding off towards the nearest side-door. 'We're going to the churchyard.'

There was no moon. A smothering thicket of snow-clouds capped the impenetrable darkness of the night, and a flake or two drifted down hither and thither as Theo stood over Lord Felix's grave.

The plot was in a sorry state. Lord Werth had made a mess of it already, when he had first dug up his predecessor. Lord Felix's subsequent habit of popping in and out of his coffin had rendered it futile to fill the grave back in, and months of wind and rain had turned the neat pile of turned earth into a half-frozen morass of mud. Some of it had fallen in upon the weathered lid of Felix's coffin, though not enough to bury him again.

69

Theo reached down with the blade of his axe, and thumped the head of it against the frost-coated wood. 'Lord Felix!' he called. 'Are you awake?'

Nothing stirred.

Theo hesitated. He was not perfectly certain how his father's dark arts worked. Once raised, was a corpse forever reanimated, in an imperfect semblance of restored life? Felix's extended period of activity suggested as much. Then again, Lord Werth had seemed displeased, and sometimes taken aback, to find Felix out of his grave and wandering the park, which implied that he had not quite expected it.

'If no one has seen Felix for weeks, does that mean he is dead again?' Theo asked of the empty air — or of Great-Uncle Silvester, though the chances of receiving a useful response from either were approximately equal. 'Actually dead? Reduced to an inanimate bundle of bones?'

If it did, then Theo was out of luck, at least until Christmas was over and Lord Werth returned.

Again, he extended his axe. *Thud, thud.* 'Lord Felix!' he called, louder this time. 'The family has need of you.'

Nothing happened, and since the snow was falling faster and thicker, Theo's mind wandered back to his beloved library, and that glass of brandy Silvester had mentioned. He turned away.

Thud, thud.

'Silvester?' said Theo, turning sharply back towards the dark maw of the grave. 'Is that you?'

A creak; the coffin lid lifted. '*Damn*, but it's cold,' came a rasping voice. 'What can you mean by getting me up in the dead of winter?'

'Felix?' Theo beheld a pale, haggard visage scowling up at him, and held a hand down to his ancestor. 'Devilish glad to reach you!' he said.

A decayed hand clasped his own; Theo hauled his erstwhile lordship out of his grave.

'Frost suits you,' added Theo, for the putrid, leathery

face had turned white like the ice, losing some of its off-putting qualities.

'It does *not*,' said Lord Felix, revolted. He stamped about in a circle, shaking himself and muttering something Theo did not catch. 'This had better be important,' he grumbled, returning to Theo. 'If *you* do not see the benefits of sleeping through the winter, *I* do.'

'It may be important,' said Theo. 'It may not be. That's what I'd like to determine.'

'What niffy-naffy, namby-pamby logic is that?'

'It's about the—'

'If that's all you've hauled me out of bed for, I'm going back in.'

'—the *Books*,' bellowed Theo, with due emphasis.

Lord Felix, having set one bony leg back into the depths of his vacated grave, froze. 'Was that a plural?' he said softly.

'There are two of them,' said Theo. 'They are never quiet anymore; the Book has tried *twice* to kill me in recent weeks; and they whisper together all the night long.'

'Oh, that's bad,' said Lord Felix. 'That's very bad.'

Away went any faint hopes Theo might have harboured for a breezy dismissal of his concerns. 'Do you know what they whisper about?' he said urgently. 'They speak in a language I've never heard.'

'What possessed any of you to bring another one out here? Have you *no* sense?'

'Believe me, sir, I have been regretting it these several weeks.'

Lord Felix looked wildly about. 'They are not nearby, are they?'

'Heavens, no. They're in the cellar.'

'Oh! Then that's all right.' He stretched out his arms, shooting back the cuffs of his mouldy velvet coat (one of Lord Werth's better garments, until recently). 'You have never learned how to talk to it, have you?' he said. 'Did not even know of the Assembly, until *I* took the matter in hand! I'd better have a look.'

'I got it to give up the ritual,' protested Theo, feeling obscurely injured by this adverse reflection on his Book-management capabilities.

But Lord Felix shook his head. Snow thickly crusted his matted dark hair. 'Haven't got the knack,' he said, loping off towards the looming shadow of the Towers. 'Better let me have a look.'

'You'll want the axe,' Theo called after him, but undeath lent an unnatural speed to Felix's feet (Theo supposed), for the disreputable old lord proved impossible to catch. Theo did not draw level with him again until he had plunged back into the shadowy Towers and wended his way back to the cellar staircase.

Lord Felix was then at the bottom of it. Silvester sat atop a door-frame once again, but he had fluttered down into the bowels of the earth, and crouched now atop the portal behind which the Book of Werth lay. The two of them maintained an unearthly silence.

Theo stopped at the bottom of the steps, and waited.

The Books were in full flow, and Theo was not reassured to discern a degree of snarling amongst the whispers. Felix stood in an odd posture, as though he had been on the point of unbolting the door and going in, only to freeze halfway through this process. His hands were raised, his head tilted, one foot half lifted. He did not move for some minutes, and all through this peculiar moment the whispering went on.

At last, he spoke.

'They are speaking English,' he said, abandoning his strange pose, and dusting a clod of earth from his sleeve. 'But they are speaking an archaic form of it, and at such speed it is difficult to follow.'

'You understand them?' said Theo.

'Not very much,' Felix admitted. 'But one or two words are clear enough.'

'Such as?' prompted Theo, with some impatience,

when his lordship paused.

'The word "Wyrde", for one. And that ought to come as no surprise, for is not the word itself archaic?'

'To be sure, but why are *they* bandying it about?'

'The topic is of some interest to them, obviously.' Felix lifted off the heavy oak beam that barred the door, and held out his hand. 'Axe,' he said.

Theo put the axe into Felix's hand. 'If it is, they have no love for the Wyrde,' he said. 'They are violent almost without exception.'

'Almost?' Felix paused, again in that unnatural stillness, and directed at Theo a look of enquiry.

'Mother and Gussie spoke of a Beatrice. Nell's talked to her. She says she and the Book were fast friends, until one day the thing turned aggressive. And something of the same sort seems to have happened to Gussie, though she has not been given so much opportunity to get acquainted with the thing.'

'Intriguing.' Lord Felix set the key into the lock, and as he turned it, he said: 'I believe I have deciphered what it is the Book is saying.'

Without further speech, he pushed open the door, ran inside in a great rush, and with a single throw of startling accuracy, he embedded the axe's glinting blade in the Book's aged leather cover.

The Book howled.

'And that is,' he continued, as Theo hurried inside and slammed shut the door behind him. '"Thou Shalt Rive into small Parts all those Called to the Wyrde".'

'Oh, *shalt* thou?' growled Theo, glaring at the Book.

'Not that I ever heard it say anything before,' said Felix calmly. He glanced about the shadowed room, though surely to little effect, for the lamp Theo carried emitted only light enough to dimly illuminate the table.

'What else does it say?' said Theo.

'Nothing. Just that, over and over.' He leaned over the Book and stroked the stained, dark leather of its front cover, smiling horribly. 'You remember me, do not you? We have often had converse together, you and I. Though it was always *I* who did the talking. What can you mean by such a grotesque utterance, hm? Is it the other one that's set you a-chatter?'

Theo maintained a prudent station not far from the exit, watching Lord Felix's antics with widened eyes. 'Well, but you are already dead,' he observed. 'Nothing now can kill *you*, can it?'

'Exactly so,' said Lord Felix cheerfully. 'Though I should enjoy a throttling about as much as the next person. Take the axe.'

Theo wrenched the weapon free of the skewered Book, and hefted it. He felt better with it in his hands, though the sight of the rend in the front cover growing over and disappearing contributed nothing to his comfort.

Lord Felix opened up the Book, with a degree of impunity Theo beheld with astonishment. 'Now, from where did you get that nasty little line?' he said, frowning. 'Show me.' These latter words he spoke in a grim tone, a decided order, though his gestures remained gentle — almost affectionate.

The Book made no response, at first. Then a page slowly turned, and another, and then many pages flew by in a blur.

'Ah,' said Lord Felix softly, and set the tip of one finger to the revealed page.

Cautiously, Theo joined him at the table, and bent to look.

"***Thou Shalt Rive into small Parts all those Called to the Wyrde.***"

'Now, I might be mistaken,' said Lord Felix, with the happy insouciance of one who imagines nothing of the kind, 'but I believe this is the very first page.'

'Charming sentiment,' muttered Theo. 'But who wrote it in there?'

'An excellent question.'

'And what in damnation is the thing doing at the Towers, if that's how it feels?'

'Also a superb question. Really, Theodore, you surprise me.'

'Thought me a dullard, did you?'

'The notion had crossed my mind. I apologise, my boy, truly I do.'

Theo, detecting a certain satire in the words, scowled.

'Well, Bookins?' said Lord Felix sweetly. 'Shall we have a new question?' He stroked the page, smiling as the threatening words were limned, briefly, in fire. Then, a grim authoritarian again in a flash, he barked: 'Who made you?'

The Book trembled, and emitted a tearing shriek.

'Stop that ghastly noise!' Felix thundered. 'Or I shall let Theo at you with the axe.'

'Good god,' said Theo faintly. 'Is it... *frightened?*'

'Everything living feels fear, Theodore,' said Lord Felix, in a gloating tone.

'But is the thing living?'

'It is capable of movement, of action, and — to a certain extent — of sentiments. And it is capable of fear. To all intents and purposes, then, we may conclude that it lives.' To the Book, he spoke again. 'Who made you?' The words this time emerged softly, silkily, and he stroked the pages once more.

A page turned. A frontispiece appeared, printed in black ink upon a page of exquisite, creamy vellum, only a little yellowed with age.

Cruikshank & Wirt
Gleucestre

'I stand corrected,' said Lord Felix. '*This* is the very first page.'

'What does it mean?' said Theo, staring at the strange names. 'Gleucestre — that must mean Gloucester, I

75

imagine, but who are Cruikshank and Wirt?'

'You're the scholar, are not you?' said Lord Felix, closing the Book with a *thump*. 'That is for you to discover.'

EIGHT

To Gussie's mild horror, she later found Clarissa Selwyn cosied up in the library with Miss Frostell.

The two had a dragon-sized bowl of custard between them. They had pulled two of Lord Maundevyle's better armchairs up to the fire — only two feet separated them from a fiery doom — and sat happily with spoons in hand, taking mouthfuls of the creamy stuff and gossiping.

Gussie knew them to be gossiping when their conversation ceased abruptly the moment she entered the room.

In Miss Frostell's eye she detected traces of guilt.

'My dear!' said that lady, upon beholding her erstwhile protégé. 'You must be perished with cold! Here, have my seat.' She bustled out of the chair in question as she spoke, relinquishing the bowl into Miss Selwyn's sole care.

'Now I *know* you to be overcome with remorse,' said Gussie, venturing in, but eschewing the proffered seat. 'Come, let me have the worst of it. What have you two been saying about me?'

'I have only been telling Miss Selwyn how *brave* you've been,' said Miss Frostell, and licked a stray morsel of custard from her spoon.

'Over the Book? But I haven't,' said Gussie. 'At

present, you could not pay me to be in the same room with it.'

'I was speaking of your Wyrde, my dear, and how startling it has all been for you. And how *trying!* Now, I know it has been, though it is like your good nature to disclaim.'

Gussie had, in fact, been disclaiming, but here she stopped. 'Good nature!' she crowed. 'Do you hear that, Miss Selwyn? Only someone *very* fond of me indeed could think me capable of that, and therefore you are forgiven, Frosty.'

Perceiving a charming look of utter bewilderment in Miss Frostell's smiling face, Gussie elaborated: 'In speaking of my Wyrde to Miss Selwyn, you are betraying all my secrets. I had hoped to maintain a certain air of mystique, you know.'

'Oh, but I know all about it already,' said Miss Selwyn carelessly. 'If I could get Mama to *stop* speaking of it, I should be very well pleased. How have you managed to avoid her, by the by? I imagined she would have you nailed to the spot by now, bound to listen to every one of her deplorable notions.'

'Are there a very great many?' said Gussie, concerned. 'And I thought my list of reasons to avoid her ladyship was long enough already.'

'It can only grow longer,' said Miss Selwyn, rather morosely, and returned her attention to the custard.

'And have you Wyrded her ladyship already?' said Miss Frostell, her eyes brightening. 'What has she become?'

'Are you hoping for a dragon?' said Gussie. 'That would be the heights of disloyalty, for you must know the rest of us are hoping for anything but.'

'I thought a wyvern might better suit.'

'Good gracious, no,' said Miss Selwyn, with an eloquent shudder. She had set aside her tricorne hat; Gussie perceived it, set carefully aside upon a low table. 'Can you imagine Mama, armed with sharp teeth as well as acid words? There would never again be a moment's peace.' She looked directly at Gussie, and continued: 'If it is true that you can determine the *manner* of a person's Wyrde, I beseech you to choose something harmless.'

'You misunderstand the nature of the Wyrde,' said Gussie. 'There is no such thing as *harmless*. Every single one of us is a walking disaster.'

Clarissa's head tilted; she thought. 'Then I have changed my mind. I believe I *would* like to be Wyrded, after all.' She dropped her spoon into the bowl, and held out her hand. 'Would you be so darling as to try again? I should be much obliged to you.' She smiled. 'And for me, you must please to choose something perfectly *horrible*.'

Gussie picked up the discarded spoon, took the outstretched hand, and set the utensil into it. 'You had much better eat,' she said. 'Before Frosty devours the lot. She is partial to custard above all things.'

'Crème anglaise,' murmured Miss Selwyn, taking a spoonful.

'In truth, I think I cannot help you. To the best of my knowledge I can't choose a Wyrde-curse; whatever happens, happens without my conscious direction. But I can tell you, with reasonable certainty, that I can't bestow a Wyrde-curse where there is not potential for one. Otherwise our dear Frosty would have been Wyrde-burdened long ago.'

'Perhaps she is,' said Miss Selwyn, with a considering look at the former governess. 'You were perfectly ignorant as to your own Wyrde until recently, weren't you, Miss Werth? And you must be, what, six and twenty?'

Gussie ignored the abominable rudeness of anybody's speculating about her age. 'But others had their suspicions,' she said. 'There were signs, even if I myself was unaware of them. I don't believe anybody has ever noticed anything amiss with Frosty.'

Miss Frostell, for some reason, blushed, and delved back into the custard bowl.

'So there must be the proper lineage, at least,' Gussie continued. 'And some unnameable thing otherwise, that determines which of a given family line will emerge Wyrded, and which not.'

'Except among the Werths, where everybody is Wyrded,' said Miss Selwyn. 'Agreeably well-scheduled, too, for it is always the third birthday, I believe?'

Gussie eyed Miss Frostell askance. 'You *have* been talkative, haven't you?'

'That I heard from Mama,' said Miss Selwyn. 'She has been full of it for years. Why is it always the third birthday, Miss Werth?'

'Nobody knows. Really, if you have sought our acquaintance in the belief that we could educate you, you must be sorely disappointed.'

Miss Selwyn sighed. 'You had better find Mama, and get it over with,' she recommended. 'She will not rest until you have either made a dragon of her, or proved her incapable of it.'

'Quite right,' said Gussie. 'While I do that, pray do something useful between the two of you. We came in search of a badly-behaved Book, likely of some antiquity, and possessed of homicidal tendencies. If there is, or has ever been, such a creature at Starminster, I beg you will discover it.' With which words she left the library, emerging back into the chill of the corridor beyond. She wrapped her thick woollen shawl more closely around herself, and wandered along, lost in thought.

Lady Margery had not, despite her threats, abandoned the civilised world immediately. Perhaps it was the prospect of another sumptuous meal that detained her, or perhaps she was caught, in spite of herself, by the problem of the Books. She had asked Gussie and Lady Werth a great many questions about the two of them, and listened to their answers with avid interest. Gussie had enjoyed some hopes that she might, by the end of it, have some more insights to share, but sadly she had not. She had only curled herself up into a tight (if enormous) ball, and fallen into a rumbling slumber.

'It may take some time to sleep off so handsome a repast,' Gussie had said to Lord Maundevyle. 'We had better amuse ourselves elsewhere for a week or two.'

Where his lordship might presently be amusing himself, she did not know. Great-Aunt Honoria had, likewise, vanished, muttering something about an exploring party. Gussie might have joined her with relish, in hope of unearthing just such a Book as she sought; but, not being herself a phantasm, she was incapable of dissolving through walls, and knew her aunt would contrive better without her. Besides, Miss Selwyn was right: it was time to discharge her obligation to Lady Maundevyle, come what may of it. At least the matter would be finished with, and the dowager out of her hair.

She found her seated in her receiving-parlour, crouched there like some manner of spider, her smile indicating she had been lying in wait for just this moment. She was excessively well-dressed, as she had been every day of Gussie's visit; today she wore sapphires, and a gown of silver net over ivory silk.

'Miss Werth,' said she as Gussie entered the room. 'Dare I hope...?'

'As I said before, I believe we should conduct this experiment outdoors,' said Gussie. 'It is cold, but you will not damage the house again, should you turn Wyrded in any very *large* way.'

Her ladyship's smile suggested she anticipated the prospect with glee. 'Let us go into the park,' said she. 'We will not be in Lady Margery's way out there, and there is nothing to damage that will be much worth the regret.'

Gussie, wondering whether her son might agree with her on that point, did not choose to argue. It wasn't her house, and it wasn't her problem. She followed the dowager out into the frost-thick park, pausing to collect a thick pelisse, bonnet and gloves along the way.

81

Lady Maundevyle, tireless despite both age and cold, marched decisively out into a clear space some distance from the main body of the house. Surrounded as they were only by ice-whitened grass and an occasional bare-branched tree, Gussie judged herself safe to proceed.

'I feel bound to ask,' she said, stripping off one of her gloves. 'Are you quite, quite certain about this? I warn you, not one of us knows of a way to remove the Wyrde, once it has set in.'

'I need not grace such an absurdity with an answer,' said the dowager.

'Very well. Let us, then, proceed.' She extended her hand, free of gloves, to Lady Maundevyle, who clasped it in a bone-creaking grip, her eyes alight with anticipation.

'I do feel the process is a little underwhelming,' said Gussie by way of conversation. To be standing holding hands with the dowager in perfect silence would be far too peculiar. 'There should be some showy thing happening to mark the transformation, should not there? A shower of sparks, perhaps, or a rosy glow.'

'Lady Mary Selwyn could have obliged us,' said the dowager. 'She was my great-great-aunt, you know, a few times removed. She was said to call up fire whenever she wished, and quite out of nowhere.'

'I am sure she was a pleasure to know, and a still greater pleasure to argue with.'

'I should not mind having her Wyrde, come to think of it,' said Lady Maundevyle reflectively. 'Not so spectacular as a dragon, nor so powerful, but good in its way.'

'What exactly is it you wish to do with your Wyrde?' Gussie asked, curiosity rearing its head in spite of her best efforts. Did the woman *need* a spectacularly powerful Wyrde, after all? Would not any Wyrde-curse be enough?

'What may *not* one do, with a dragon's powers?' came the answer.

'Your son does not appear to be doing much of anything with them.' She thought, and corrected herself,

'No, that is not true. He has obligingly flown us about, some once or twice, which was useful indeed.'

Lady Maundevyle's nose wrinkled with distaste. 'I should do a great deal more, I can tell you.'

'Such as? I hope you are not planning to terrorise the villagers. It does not do to make oneself unpopular with the neighbours, I assure you.'

Lady Maundevyle bared her teeth. 'I should pay a call upon those who presume to impose a *license* scheme upon us. They would soon change their minds.'

'I rather think that would have the opposite effect,' said Gussie. 'The scheme came about because of similar behaviour, after all.'

'Then I shall eat the minister.'

'They'll appoint a new one.'

'I shall eat him, too.'

'Happy thoughts indeed,' said Gussie politely, and withdrew her hand, though with some difficulty, for Lady Maundevyle's fingers were twined tightly about her own. 'If anything is to come of this meeting, the work must now be done. I shall return to the house, where it's warmer.'

'But — are you perfectly certain that it is complete?'

'Not in the least. I haven't a notion what occurs between me and a freshly-Wyrded soul, and I cannot feel it happening, so I cannot tell you whether it's finished. You will just have to wait.'

Lady Maundevyle gave a short, angry sigh, and began to pace in circles, the cold and her irritation turning her gait straight-backed and stiff-legged.

'If we consider the example of your sons,' said Gussie, 'the process is not like to take more than half an hour.'

She turned to leave, for it was far too cold to stand about nursing my lady through her impatience. But she had not gone more than a dozen yards before she heard a shriek; unmistakeably a scream of joy, not fear.

'Something is happening!' Lady Maundevyle gasped.

Gussie felt a certain sinking at heart. She had

harboured hopes that the dowager might develop some insignificant Wyrde, of no very dangerous character. She would be angry, to be sure, but she would also be rendered (relatively) harmless; and Gussie need not consider her anger of any relevance whatsoever, once she and her family were restored to the Towers.

She did not want to turn around, and confirm with her own eyes that these hopes were unfounded. What if she saw the dragon-wings sprouting from the dowager's back, her teeth lengthening and sharpening, her body growing to monstrous size? Like it or not, *she* must bear some responsibility for any havoc the dowager might wreak in such a state; she could not achieve it without Gussie's help.

But Gussie was made of stern stuff after all, and could not dither long. She turned back, steeled herself for disaster, and fixed her eyes upon Lady Maundevyle's transforming person.

'Oh,' said she, and for a moment her mouth hung open in surprise.

Then she began to laugh.

'I do not see why it is in the least amusing,' said the dowager crossly.

'No, I don't suppose you do,' Gussie gasped. For Lady Maundevyle had not become a dragon, and she was in no wise pleased about this development.

She had, however, undergone a significant change. It was her legs that were the most altered, in that they had vanished altogether. In their place, the dowager viscountess had a fish's tail, sleek and scaled, and presently thrashing with temper.

'How *glad* I am that Aunt Wheldrake is not by!' said Gussie, smiling broadly. 'She would be ready to gut you on the spot out of pure envy.'

'A mermaid,' retorted the dowager in disgust. 'Of what possible use to me is that?'

She did not make an especially attractive mermaid. Aunt Wheldrake's fancies of abundant hair and sea-jewels were nowhere in evidence. She had retained, largely, her own torso and hair, though the latter hung in bedraggled, sea-tossed tendrils all tangled with seaweed. Her teeth, bared in a grimace that was in no way a smile, showed themselves sharp and pointed and far too numerous, like the teeth of certain fish Gussie had seen in one or another of Theo's books. Her tail, meanwhile, bore none of the prismatic colours that legend liked to describe. It was a flat, unembellished grey, like a fish.

'And lo, her ladyship transformed,' Gussie chortled to herself. 'Like a haddock out of a nightmare.'

Lady Maundevyle snarled something, and tore, most unhelpfully, at her hair.

'Well, I perceive that my work is indeed done,' said Gussie cheerfully, and turned back in the direction of the house. 'Pray excuse me! Many other calls of a similar nature to make.' And away she strode, unaffected by the dowager's vituperation except for a renewed desire to laugh.

She spared a glance or two for her own hands as she walked, agreeably surprised — and not a little discomfited — by the outcome of the morning's experiment. It had happened faster than ever, this time, and there could be no doubt that the touch of her own skin had wrought the change in the dowager. How it had happened, though, remained as much a mystery as ever. Gussie had felt nothing at all.

Still, that she was as much of a walking catastrophe as any of her peers could no longer stand in any doubt.

Heartily pleased, Gussie whistled a jaunty tune as she walked.

Upon re-entering the house, however, she found it apparently devoid either of her family or the dowager's. Nobody occupied the library, or her ladyship's favourite parlour. Gussie wandered through several of the more prominent public rooms without finding any trace of her aunt and uncle, or of Clarissa and Miss Frostell. Great-Aunt Honoria was likewise nowhere in evidence, though Gussie supposed her to be buried somewhere in the bowels of the labyrinthine house, deep in investigative bliss.

Upon querying a passing liveried footman, she learned that Lord Werth was understood to have gone outside with Benjamin (whom Gussie gathered to be the footman assigned to his lordship's use); that her aunt had retired to her bedchamber; and that Miss Selwyn and her own Miss Frostell were 'Somewhere about the house, ma'am.'

'I imagine they will be very hungry when they have finished,' Gussie said. 'Searching a house this size is like to take *some* time, after all. If you would be so good as to ask the cook to prepare another bowl of crème anglaise, we shall all be very well pleased.'

The footman bowed, and went away to carry out this request. Gussie prepared herself for a lengthy ramble up and down staircases, around winding passages, and into long-forgotten rooms, until she should either stumble upon Miss Frostell, or make some interesting discovery of her own.

The house was certainly larger than she remembered, though likely not (she admitted with some regret) because it had actually grown. More likely that her imagination had quietly shrunk the place in her memory, too appalled by the monstrosity's size to remember it clearly. After half an hour — if it was not rather more — of clambering about, her legs ached with the quantity of stairs, and she had walked into more clouds of dust and cobwebs than she cared to count.

In the end, she encountered not Miss Selwyn and her governess, but Lord Maundevyle.

She discovered him by the simple expedient of walking full-tilt into his striding person, as she turned a corner at a pace her aunt might have (fairly) censured as unwise.

'I beg your pardon!' said Gussie, retiring to a distance

of two feet from his lordship. 'I was not attending to where I was going.'

'Hoydenish behaviour, to be sure, but I believe there is no damage,' said Lord Maundevyle, making some show of inspecting himself for harm.

'But since you are here,' Gussie pursued. 'Would you mind telling me where the deuce I am?'

He blinked at this, probably disconcerted by the turn of phrase for which Gussie would not at all apologise. 'Where?' he said. 'You are a short distance from my rooms, ma'am, in that direction.' He pointed behind himself. 'And you have come from the vicinity of the royal drawing-rooms.'

'Royal!' said Gussie. 'Good heavens, are you then in the habit of entertaining their various highnesses?'

'No. But my mother lives in hope.'

'I see.'

'So did my grandmother before her.'

'It has been a long wait, has it?'

'A few generations, I believe. There is talk of the first George having once attended a dinner here, but between you and I, I am not perfectly certain it isn't a piece of fiction.'

'Well, and why not?' said Gussie. 'Whatever of honour and distinction cannot be got in reality is easily acquired by dint of a few lies.'

'I ought to have known that would be your view of it. Do you mind if I ask what *you* are doing up here, and looking like that?'

'Looking like—?' Gussie put her hands up to her hair, and drew them away with a quantity of dusty cobwebs clinging to her fingers. 'I look exactly like Great-Aunt Honoria! Charming! Though I am a little before my time.'

'You look nothing like her. Nor shall you, for another fifty years at least.'

'Then I shall get in a little practice in advance. It's always good to be prepared.' Gussie swept the worst of the

87

cobwebs from her hair, and devoted herself to the subsequent business of peeling them off her fingers. 'Dratted stuff,' she complained. 'I used to think my aunt wore them for decorative purposes, but I am now persuaded they are the product of her exploring adventures. She's stuck with them.'

'Perhaps a lady's maid assigned to her use?' suggested Lord Maundevyle.

'It's been tried. They've a tendency to run away in fits of the terrors, and my aunt laughing uproariously all the while.' She resorted to the shameful expedient of wiping her hands on the skirt of her gown. 'To answer your question, I am come up here in search of that very lady. Also your sister, and my governess. Though having seen something of the extent of your property, I am afraid we shall never see any of them ever again. They must be entirely lost.'

'Clarissa knows her way about. I cannot answer for your aunt, however. She will be forced to haunt us forever.'

'Nothing is like to please her better.'

'May I walk with you? Perhaps if we join forces, we might discover them after all.'

'It might help if one of us knows his way about,' she agreed, permitting him to fall into step beside her. 'By the by, if you are at all interested in the question of your mother's whereabouts, I believe I may help you there.'

'I perceive mischief behind this seemingly innocuous question,' said he, looking into her face. 'You are trying not to smile, and not getting on very well at it.'

Gussie chuckled. 'Rejoice, for she has got her wish! Your very amiable Miss Werth having cheerfully wreaked havoc once again.'

'Both times by request,' he reminded her.

'Not in your case.'

'I've forgiven you. What is it that you've done to Mother?'

'She's become a creature of the seas.'

'A what?' He stopped dead in surprise. 'Never tell me you've turned her into a fish.'

'A nymph of the waters,' Gussie persevered. 'Delicate and wave-tossed, a veritable delight upon the eyes—'

'A mermaid?' he said, thunderstruck. 'No! *Really?*'

Gussie, unable to help herself, began again to laugh. 'Yes, but not at all as you are picturing it, I am certain. No, no, do not ask me to describe her. This is a vision you must enjoy with your own eyes.'

Lord Maundevyle eyed her askance, and began again to walk. 'I look forward to it. You intrigue me excessively.'

'She is not happy.'

'Do not let that trouble you. Nothing short of dragonhood was like to please her, and that was never very likely.'

'Two dragons in the same family is far too much to expect,' Gussie agreed. '*One* being, of course, perfectly reasonable.'

He smiled at that. 'I'd give her my Wyrde-curse in a heartbeat, if I could.'

'No!' cried Gussie, appalled. 'Never do that! Can you imagine the trouble she would cause?'

'It's all right. I cannot think it will ever be possible anyway.'

'You'd think not, but what *I* do is not commonly held to be possible either.'

'There is that.'

They had ambled some little distance by this time, though Gussie, amused by the conversation, had ignored all of the doors that opened off the panelled walls of the corridor. She now halted, and held up a hand to cut off his lordship's next words, for a faint sound had reached her ears.

The distant sound of tramping feet, coming nearer, and a voice she recognised as Miss Selwyn's.

Then came Miss Frostell's voice in answer, too far away

yet for Gussie to discern what they were saying.

'I believe we have found two of our lost souls,' said she. 'Or, they are about to find us.'

So it proved, for upon turning another corner Gussie beheld the pair of them, hastening along in high gig, Miss Frostell's enthusiasm and energy making her almost as youthful as her companion. 'Aha!' cried she, upon espying Gussie. 'Excellent! We have something of *very* great import to tell you, my dear!' She made her curtsey to Lord Maundevyle, smiling rosily, and he returned the salutation with a bow.

'Miss Frostell,' he said. 'Clarissa. How relieved we are to find you still among the living.'

Miss Selwyn, wearing her tricorne hat again, together with a mischievous smile, said: 'Among the living, Henry? You cannot imagine me to be in any danger in my own house, surely?'

'You'd be surprised,' Gussie muttered, thinking of the Book, and Theo.

Lord Maundevyle's mouth twitched at this, his thoughts no doubt following Gussie's. 'Miss Werth was afraid you might have lost yourselves in our maze of a house,' he explained.

'Afraid?' said Miss Frostell. 'My dear Miss Werth? Forgive me, my lord, but you must be mistaken.'

'Yes, I was not very much discomposed by the idea,' Gussie admitted. 'Lord Maundevyle gives me graces I do not possess.'

'Let us term it confidence in our intrepid explorers' abilities,' suggested he.

'That is respectable,' Gussie agreed. 'Far more so than a heartless lack of interest in their welfare, no? Well, Frosty, and now comes your moment. I hope you plan to shock me very thoroughly.'

'I believe I might, at that,' said Miss Frostell. 'But since it was Miss Selwyn's discovery, she ought rightly to have the telling of it.'

'It's a book,' said Miss Selwyn, in a tone Gussie might almost have termed bored. 'That is what you were looking for, isn't it?'

'A book? Just that?' said Gussie. 'That is not perfectly true, for I've already perceived that your library contains a quantity of them.'

'Yes, but a *strange* book,' said Miss Selwyn. 'Though in point of fact it isn't a real book, only a picture of one.'

This interested Gussie rather more. 'Pray describe it?'

'No, no, my dear,' said Miss Frostell. 'You must come with us, and see it for yourself.'

Away they bustled, Gussie and Lord Maundevyle with them. Back through the house they went, in a journey of some few minutes. It ended at last in a passage Gussie did, distantly, recall, for she had passed down it before: on her previous visit to Starminster, when Great-Uncle Silvester had drawn her attention to the existence of a prodigious gallery of paintings.

Here they were again.

'Good God, I have been a fool!' said she, thunderstruck. 'I knew of the family paintings, of course, but it had not entered my head to look for a record of the Book among them.' Nor had she noticed such a thing before, but then, she had not been thinking of the Book of Werth at the time. Her mind had been occupied by her own predicament.

Miss Selwyn went into the gallery without another word, throwing the doors open wide. She trod at a bruising pace near to the other side of the room, and stood before one of the larger paintings in the collection, Miss Frostell trailing eagerly at her heels. 'Here it is,' she said. 'It looks like nothing of note to me, but your Miss Frostell thinks otherwise.'

Gussie caught up, and stood in scrutiny. The painting was immense, daubed in oils upon a thick canvas, and bordered in a wrought golden monstrosity of a frame. Depicted within was a gentleman who had, by his attire, lived several centuries before. Nothing about the man himself interested Gussie very much; he was plain of feature, and well into his middle years, with thinning hair ill-disguised by a velvet cap. Nothing about him suggested he bore any particular Wyrde, though that, of course, meant nothing; many Wyrde-curses were invisible to the eye.

What *did* interest her was the book he held.

It was partly his posture. He clasped the thing to his torso, his hold almost an embrace, despite the size and probable weight of the thing. Thick and cumbersome, with ornate hinges, it had leather covers tinted dark green, and was inscribed with golden lettering Gussie could not read.

'That's it,' she gasped. 'The Book of Maundevyle. It has to be.'

'Is not it?' said Miss Frostell. 'I knew it must be of significance, the moment I saw it.'

'Do you know who this is?' Gussie said, addressing her question to the Selwyn siblings.

Both of them appeared at a loss. 'Not really,' said Miss Selwyn. 'Some ancestor. I am sure he is not at all worth remembering.'

'Possibly a former Lord Maundevyle,' said the current one. 'He has the look of it.'

He did indeed sport a certain pomposity about him, bestowed, perhaps, by the smirksome curl to his smile, and the obvious pride with which he wore his sumptuous clothing. Plainly an aristocrat.

She searched the painting for anything else that might offer some clue. In particular, any sign that the book clutched in Lord Maundevyle's feverish grip might, in fact, have been a *Book*. There was nothing.

'I cannot decide,' said she. 'It could be any sort of book. There is nothing to suggest—'

She broke off, for her perceptive eye had noticed a peculiarity about the painting after all. A cunningly disguised trick, almost a trompe l'oeil, so carefully daubed by the painter as to escape all but the most determined scrutiny.

'Look,' she breathed, and pointed.

The book — no, the *Book* — had appendages. A great many of them. In point of fact, everything in the picture, save only the aristocrat's face and hands, was made up of them. They formed the velvet of his sleeves, and the coiled contours of his cap; they made up the legs of a table positioned at his elbow, and a second, painted frame positioned inside the outer, gold-fashioned one.

If Gussie read the image correctly, the Book had swallowed everything in the painting. And its subject was in no way discomposed by the fact.

'Interesting,' said Miss Selwyn. 'How perceptive of you, Miss Werth. I had never before noticed that.'

'Nor I,' admitted Lord Maundevyle. 'But then we have had nothing like Miss Werth's motive to look closely.'

'Or information,' said Gussie. 'Had I perceived this effect a few months ago, I would probably have discounted its importance. Only *now* does it strike me as a significant oddity.'

'He appears to be fond of it,' said Miss Frostell, in a tone of wonder. 'How can that be possible?'

'Unaccountable,' Gussie agreed. 'But he is like Aunt Beatrice in that. I wonder if this fellow was ever savaged by the thing?'

'Or if he minded?' said Miss Selwyn, her eyes brightening. 'I like a man who can stand a good savaging.'

'Then we must find you such a man,' said Gussie. 'But one who is both alive, and not a relative, by preference.'

Miss Selwyn turned her gaze upon Gussie, with a significance Gussie had no trouble in reading.

'Theo is not on the market,' she said.

'He's single.'

'And unmarriageable. Really, I'd encourage you to forget about him.'

'I await your alternative suggestions with the greatest

anticipation.'

Gussie blinked. 'I am no matchmaker.'

'Then you should not have said *we*, should you?'

Gussie controlled a desire to throttle the girl, and turned back to the painting. 'What I'd like to know,' she said firmly, 'is: where is that Book now?'

'Somewhere about the place, no doubt,' said Miss Selwyn. 'You would hardly believe the quantity of nonsense we have lying about in corners, gathering dust.'

'I'd be surprised if this proved a part of it,' said Gussie, brushing gentle fingers over the painted representation of the Book. 'Your mama claims there is no such thing in the possession of your family.'

'And since she is known far and wide for the strict truth of her every utterance, there can be no possibility of mistake,' said Miss Selwyn.

'Why, that was a sarcasm worthy of your own wit, my dear,' said Miss Frostell, looking upon the other young woman with admiration. 'How fortunate that the two of you have become friends!'

Miss Werth and Miss Selwyn eyed one another, Gussie with some ill-concealed feelings of resentment, and Clarissa with a seraphic smile.

'Do you indeed think your mother might have lied about that?' said Gussie, choosing to let this well-meant effusion pass.

'Mama is secretive by nature,' said Miss Selwyn. 'I don't believe she would ever give away information, unless forced.'

'But neither of you have ever seen or heard of such a Book in these parts?' This question she addressed to both the Selwyn siblings, and to her dismay both of them were quick to agree.

'I've never found such a thing in our library,' said Lord Maundevyle.

'The servants have never mentioned anything of the like,' said Miss Selwyn, which was compelling as an argument, for what the servants did not know was not, as a rule, worth the knowing.

'So it isn't here anymore,' said Gussie thoughtfully. 'Perhaps it no longer exists; many a Werth has harboured a fervent desire to destroy *ours*. But I'm intrigued to know that we are not the only Wyrded family in England who once owned such a Book. I wonder why?'

Great-Aunt Honoria's voice emanated from the empty air a ways behind Gussie. 'I couldn't say, but I can tell you something else.'

Gussie whirled about, but caught no glimpse of her aunt's perambulatory head. 'And are you now turned invisible?' said she. 'There is no end to your wily arts.'

Honoria gave a cackle. 'In a manner of speaking,' she said, as a quantity of flesh bled down the wall, and resolved itself into the old woman's ghoulish face. 'Only cunningly obscured, but it amounts to the same thing. Do you want to know what I've found?

'I am overpowered with curiosity,' Gussie assured her.

The head danced. 'Then come below!' she said, and began to dematerialise.

'Wait!' called Gussie. 'Below where?'

Great-Aunt Honoria clucked in disgust. 'The cellars, Augusta. Where else?'

She then vanished in earnest, leaving Gussie, Miss Frostell and the Selwyns to make their own way down the various flights of stairs and through a plethora of passageways.

When at length they reassembled in the Starminster cellars — which, to Gussie's mild resentment, were also of a size, and even a grandeur, to put those of the Towers to shame — Gussie called out: 'Well, Aunt, here we are. Where is this grand discovery of yours?'

'In here!' trilled the revenant.

She continued to sing in macabre tones as Gussie groped her way through a network of passages, with the help of the sole lamp she had been able to secure on the way down. The upper level was not too difficult to navigate, a number of half-windows permitting a dim light to filter in. But once they ventured below, the wan winter sun was extinguished, and Gussie's lamp all they had to navigate by.

'How fortunate that this should not be a hair-raising endeavour,' said she calmly. 'Or my poor Frosty will be regretting her involvement.'

Miss Frostell was, indeed, looking less than comfortable, and stayed as close to Gussie and her lamp as she could. The cellars above were white-washed and clean and organised, but the lower level had all the cold stone walls, the dank chill, the cobwebs and the distant scuttling of rats that one might associate with the very worst examples. 'I shall do very well,' said Miss Frostell, stoutly enough, but Gussie detected a quaver in her voice.

'Take heart,' she said. 'We shan't be here long. Either we will complete our errand, and go directly above; or we shall be rent apart by monsters, and insensible of further danger.'

'There are no monsters,' called Great-Aunt Honoria, with evident regret. 'Only an empty room.'

'But how disappointing,' said Gussie. 'I had expected a minotaur at the least.'

Following her aunt's voice, she arrived upon the threshold of a room every bit as decrepit as the rest. Not that the grey stone walls and floors, or the solid oak door, were in any way unsound. The chamber merely had the look of a room no one had set foot in for — possibly — decades. The floor was slippery with damp and a creeping rot, the ceiling positively festooned with a tattered, spiderish drapery.

'A charming place,' said Gussie, holding the lamp high. The dim golden glow illuminated nothing of any especial interest. 'Why is it that we're here?'

'Because of this,' said Great-Aunt Honoria, manifesting above a high table of some sort set against the back wall.

Gussie ventured nearer. 'A plinth,' she said. 'There is something familiar about it.'

'Well there might be,' said Honoria. 'Is it not much like the one upon which our own, dear Book rests?'

'You think this is where a Book was kept?'

'It looks like it, does it not?'

'It could very well be.' Gussie inspected the plinth for another moment, and then stepped away, leaving the Selwyns to their scrutiny. The thing was not in itself informative. 'You have found no trace of an actual Book, I suppose?' she said to her aunt.

'Not a one. If such a thing once lived here, it has long since escaped.'

Gussie shuddered at that prospect. An escaped Book, rampaging about the countryside and terrorising the farmers — what a nightmare.

'Let us hope it was simply burned,' she said.

'It might have been sold,' said Honoria.

'Like Mrs. Daventry's curse-book. Very true. But to whom? And where is it now?'

'Does it matter?' said Honoria indifferently. 'We have a very good Book of our own.'

'It might be a danger to the world, if not properly contained.'

If Honoria had possessed shoulders, she would have shrugged them at that.

'Never say this prospect disturbs you?' said Lord Maundevyle, turning from his own inspection of the plinth.

'It does, and I will tell you why,' said Gussie. 'Already we Wyrded are under closer watch than we used to be, because one or two wyverns could not control themselves. What if such Books as these were known to be ravening about and doing away with people, like Mrs. Daventry's? *One* such incident has done enough damage. If there are to be more, then we will find ourselves subject to more punishing schemes than this charming notion of being

97

registered, and licensed.'

'How freeing it is to be unWyrded,' said Miss Selwyn. 'I had no notion.'

'Your fate is merely to be mauled by such a Book,' said Gussie. 'I congratulate you. A simple, straightforward destiny; nothing so complicated as being tainted by association, or anything so thorny.'

'I look forward to it,' said Miss Selwyn, and with perfect truth, for all Gussie could tell. 'I anticipate a positively *hideous* death.'

But Miss Frostell gave a tiny mew of fright, and shrank away from the dark corners of the chamber.

'Done for, Frosty?' said Gussie. 'Let us go up, shall we? I do not think there is anything to be gained from lingering.'

Once restored to light, and air, and liberty, Miss Frostell soon calmed.

'I suppose we must question your mother,' said Gussie to Lord Maundevyle. 'Try if we cannot persuade her to tell us the truth about that painting.'

'Good luck with that,' said Miss Selwyn.

'If she knows anything of it,' said Lord Maundevyle. 'She may not have lied, when she claimed we had never had such a Book. She may simply be ignorant of it, as we were. You must go farther back with the Selwyns, as we did with Lady Margery.'

Gussie thought. 'Are there any freakishly long-lived dragons among your ancestors?'

'Not to my knowledge.'

'You disappoint me.'

'But,' he continued. 'Your esteemed uncle was given the run of the family plot, was not he?'

Gussie began to smile. 'Why, yes,' she said with relish. 'Yes, he was.'

NINE

'Right,' Lord Felix announced, upon emerging from the Book of Werth's cellar prison. 'If that's everything, I am going back to bed.'

'You wouldn't fancy a cup of tea first?' Theo ventured. My Lord Werth-as-was might be an infernal nuisance, but Theo felt curiously unwilling to permit him to vanish back into his grave when the problem of the Books remained unresolved. He, Theo, had boasted that he could manage the creatures better than anyone, but that was before he had seen Lord Felix attempt it.

'I cannot imagine what use you think a deadman has for tea,' said Lord Felix.

'Little more than I do, but you'll still find me partaking of a cup now and then.'

'Ladies talk you into it, do they?' said the old lord shrewdly.

'Well, yes. Come to think of it, it *is* usually when they want to *talk and talk* to me, but I assure you—'

'You'll manage fine, boy,' said Lord Felix, clapping him heartily upon the shoulder. 'You have ruthlessness enough about you, and you don't shy away from a challenge.'

Before Theo could think of a suitable way to express his feelings about this dubious vote of confidence, Lord Felix had set off at a smartish pace for the nearest exit, and was all but gone from sight.

Suppressing an unmanly sigh of dejection, Theo returned to his library. The whispering was by now becoming cursedly familiar, which made it both less disruptive and somehow more alarming at the same time. He sat before the fire and tried, really *tried,* to interest himself in a tome about the Reanimation of Persons No Longer Living, neatly thieved from his father's private collection. But while some one or two of its insights proved of interest, especially as applied to Lord Felix, Theo's mind could not help but wander back to the Book of Werth.

Eventually, he abandoned this unhelpful pursuit and took himself off to his writing-desk. Situated as this was in his own rooms at the top of the tallest of the towers, he enjoyed a charming view over the white-blanketed countryside as he penned a missive to Mr. Ballantine, of Bow Street.

I find myself unable to investigate further, he wrote at the end, having conveyed the question of Cruikshank and Wirt. *There is nothing at the Towers that might cast any light on who these people were, and what they were doing creating such a ghastly oddity. I leave it in your hands.*

This he dispatched to London with all possible speed, and settled down to await a reply.

Days passed, and no letters came. Theo spent the time in ceaselessly wandering the Towers, for the snow proved too impenetrable for him to prowl about the park as much as he normally would. He would have gone hungry, were it not for Mrs. Gosling's cheerful promptitude in preparing suitable provender for him, and having it dispatched up to his tower at regular intervals. How she came by it, he did not choose to ask.

He could settle to nothing, for the damned whispering remained at the back of his mind all night long. He hardly slept, snatching a few hours when the sun was up, and otherwise maintaining his lonely vigil over the thrice-cursed Books. Paranoia grew upon him by the day; now that their unholy purpose was confirmed, Theo could swear that they were plotting his own personal demise.

Probably they were.

The quietness of the Towers had much to do with his uncharacteristic alarm. Accustomed as he was to an irritating surplus of noise, the absence of his parents and Great-Aunt Honoria — yes, and even Gussie — left so heavy a silence in their wake that he did not know what to do with it. All manner of unwelcome ideas sprang to life in the midst of that void, confined to Theo's mind thus far, but none the less real for all that.

He began, traitorously, to wish that he had gone to Starminster after all. He could even have put up with Charles Selwyn if it meant a reprieve from the Books and their damned *whispering*.

Very late one frigid day, some nine or ten days into the family's absence from the Towers, and when Theo, observing the sinking of the sun with a similar sinking at heart, prepared himself for a renewed onslaught, there came a knock at the library door. A diffident tap, more like, so it could not herald an unlooked-for early return of his family.

'Come in?' he said.

A footman appeared, and bowed. 'Sorry to disturb you, my lord, but there's someone to see you.'

'Who is it, Oliver?' said Theo, without looking up from his reading. If it was not his mother and father come back again, he could scarcely be interested. Whoever it was would do better to turn tail and run away again.

'Says his name's Ballantine, sir, but he don't look like himself.'

And Theo looked up. 'Ballantine?' he repeated. 'What do you mean, he's not like himself?'

Oliver merely grimaced uncomfortably. 'I couldn't say, sir. You'd have to see him for yourself.'

Theo set aside his book, and got to his feet. 'Damn, man, show him in! It's perishing outside.'

The footman hesitated. 'It's just that I'm not perfectly certain it's him, sir.'

'If it's someone come to rob the place, he's welcome to it,' said Theo savagely. 'And if he's got thoughts of murdering us in our beds, he's cordially invited to have a go.'

'Yes, sir,' said Oliver, and withdrew.

Theo waited by the fire.

A few moments later, the door opened again, revealing this time a figure Theo indeed did not recognise.

But it spoke with Mr. Ballantine's gruff voice and light Scottish burr when it said: 'Aye, no pretty sight, am I?'

Theo stared in momentary speechlessness. Ballantine — if it was he — had surely not been so tall, when Theo had last met him? He certainly had not been so broad at the shoulder, nor so very muscular.

All of which might be well enough in a fine figure of a man, but there was more. Whatever pleasing symmetry of feature he might once have possessed was gone, replaced with a lumpishness no one could term attractive. What's more, he had sharp, powerful teeth; a short pair of horns protruded from the thick, black, snow-drowned curls atop his head; and his mouth was framed either side by a pair of curving tusks.

'Good god, man,' said Theo faintly. 'What in the blazes are you?'

Mr. Ballantine's smile emerged oddly around the tusks, and the teeth. 'I don't know as there's ever been a precise term coined,' he said. 'The best I've heard is "ogre". I suppose it's apt enough.'

Theo recovered his composure. 'Come in,' he said, gesturing to a chair he thought large enough to accommodate so huge a man. 'You must be freezing.'

'I am that,' Mr. Ballantine agreed, venturing into the library with a diffidence Theo had never known him to display before. 'Forgive my state. I'd never have presented myself thus, but that it's so cursed cold. I'm a lot more weather-proof like this.'

Theo cleared his throat. 'Ah. Legend has it that ogres are fond of...'

'Eating the flesh of men?' said Mr. Ballantine, with a twinkle somewhere down in those deep-set eyes. 'Why, aren't you so?'

'Not the meat,' said Theo shortly. 'And I don't, as a rule, partake of my fellow man.'

'How noble.' Mr. Ballantine lowered himself with some care into the indicated chair, which creaked under his weight, but did not collapse. 'Neither do I, as a rule.' He sat for a moment, looking at the fire. 'I ought to be able to resume my regular proportions in a little while, once I'm warm. I'd sooner do so before I see her ladyship.'

'She isn't here,' said Theo. 'No one's here but me.'

That won him a quick, dark look. 'Not here? Where should they have gone, in this weather?'

'They're all gone to Starminster for Christmas. Not back for some days yet.'

'Starminster, hm? I had thought there was no love lost between the two households.'

'Perfectly true,' Theo assured him. 'But there was something to be gained by it. Gussie wanted to see what a mess she could make of Lady Maundevyle.'

The tusks twitched. 'An unimpeachable motive.'

'Yes, wasn't it? And she had some thoughts of enquiring about the matter of the Books, too. I believe my mother and father went along to keep her out of trouble.'

'You've heard nothing as to their success?'

'Don't need to. Nothing can keep Gussie out of trouble.'

'Ah, I can't argue with that. But as to the Books?'

Theo shook his head. 'Like as not they've come up dry.'

'It's on that subject I've come north,' said Ballantine.

'As you may imagine. Those names you discovered.'

'Yes?' Theo, alert, leaned forward.

'Cruikshank is the name of a printer's and typesetter's that used to reside in the city of Gloucester,' said Ballantine. 'Many years ago now. Long defunct. Owned by one Thaddeus Cruikshank. I've sent a man to Gloucester to find out more, if he can.'

'And Wirt?'

'Well, now.' Ballantine stretched his huge hands towards the fire, and slowly turned them. 'I have my own ideas about that, but I can't tell you more just now.'

'Why not?'

'I don't choose to share what could at best be called an inchoate theory. When I have something solid, you'll be the first to know.'

'I have no objection to a man's being wrong once in a while,' said Theo, frowning.

'In this case, you might.'

Theo shrugged his shoulders, and abandoned the question. But Ballantine's presence at the Towers made him uneasy, and it was not merely the rude and uncouth shape that he presently wore. Theo eyed him. 'All this might have been put in a letter, might not it? I was expecting a response in paper only, not in person.'

Ballantine grinned, his tusks twitching horribly. 'Aye, you're right enough. I had another purpose in mind when I decided to come this far.'

Theo did not much like the pause that followed. It was a hesitation suggestive of some proposition to come, the nature of which Theo would not approve.

'I'd like to take Mrs. Daventry's book away with me,' said Ballantine after a moment.

Theo straightened. 'But that is excellent news.'

'Ah… I'm pleased you think so.' Ballantine met Theo's eyes squarely. 'But I'm concerned about its safety in transit.'

'A fair concern. What have you in mind?'

Ballantine jerked a meaty thumb over his shoulder, pointing back the way he had come. 'I have a... conveyance. It's stout enough.'

'But?' Theo said, when the Runner hesitated again.

'I don't know that I can manage the thing alone.'

Theo's brow darkened. 'And you have brought along some several sturdy fellows, no doubt, all armed to the teeth?'

'I would have, if I'd thought it would help.' His smile was rueful. 'It takes a certain experience to handle that book without anyone coming to harm. I learned that the painful way, last summer.'

'Does it,' said Theo awfully.

'And a certain attitude besides, one might say.'

'One might indeed.' Theo entertained a brief fantasy of fobbing Ballantine off with Lord Felix; the pestersome old lord was certainly equal to the task. But he soon abandoned the idea. Said pestersome old lord was also in shabby state, brittle and frail. Could he survive a long, jolting journey into London? Supposing he did, what would become of him in the midst of the capital? The general public were aware enough of the Wyrded, but to turn a walking corpse loose among them would be the outside of enough.

Mr. Ballantine was watching him with a hopeful air, in response to which Theo only frowned more deeply. 'I do not ordinarily leave the Towers,' he said.

'But you did so last summer. Twice, wasn't it?'

'Yes, but only because of Gussie's damned meddling! And the Selwyns! A cursed nuisance, the lot of them.'

'I need not detain you long in London. I've a prison prepared, and a few good men ready to receive it. I only look for help in conveying it there.'

'Why do you want it, anyway?' said Theo, unable to help sounding injured, though the removal of that second Book was exactly what he had wished for. He hadn't wanted to have to *do* anything to effect this agreeable change.

'It's hard to study a Book that's ninety miles distant. Besides, it never sat well with me to leave it here in the first place. That was a temporary measure, turned to of necessity, and it pleases me to be able to relieve you of the burden now.'

'You're aware, are you, that it's wide awake?'

'It hasn't ever gone back into dormancy?'

'No. Neither has ours. I believe they're keeping each other lively.'

'That does complicate things,' Mr. Ballantine allowed. 'Though if we wait to move it until it's sleepy again, by your account that day might never come.'

Theo subsided into thoughtful silence, brows knit. He knew Mr. Ballantine spoke sense; the curse-book ought to be removed. His father and mother would be relieved to be rid of it, as would he. And if it was going to be sent away, it ought to be done at once.

Still, he did not relish the prospect of taking it out of its cellar prison, carrying it all through the house, and actually taking it *outside*, into the driveway, where Ballantine's "conveyance" waited. How could any of that be done without the infernal thing's escaping?

'Did you bring a strong-box, by any chance?' said he at last.

'I've a box,' nodded the Runner. 'Stout steel, with a set of chains besides, and another lock-box to put it inside.'

Theo stretched, conscious of a growing tension in his muscles. 'Well then, we'd best get to it,' he said. 'The sooner it's done, the happier I will be.'

'As will I, my lord.'

'But first,' Theo added. 'I've got to go out to the graveyard.'

Ballantine's thick, bushy brows rose.

'It's complicated,' said Theo shortly.

'I'm at Werth Towers,' said Ballantine. 'Of course it's complicated.'

Ballantine insisted on accompanying Theo out to the churchyard. Theo had not the leisure to argue the point with him, his mind being too busy turning over the dual problem of removing one Book while leaving the other suitably watched in his absence.

'The only person I can ask is Lord Felix,' he explained as the two hastened along the quiet lane, moonlit by that hour, and sparkling with frost. 'The servants cannot cope with it, nor should they be expected to. And my father is not to return for several days.'

'Lord Felix,' said Ballantine. 'Is that the fellow to whose kind interference I owe my acquaintance with your family?'

'Yes,' said Theo shortly.

'And he's in the graveyard?'

'Dead people usually are.'

That silenced Ballantine, who trod along with Theo in what was probably an appalled silence.

Then again, he was part of a division of Runners whose role was to apprehend the misbehaving Wyrded; revenants and the undead must surely have crossed his path before.

'Father's work,' Theo added. 'Though I doubt he intended for Felix to be ambulatory for this long.'

'Stubborn, is he?' Ballantine nodded. 'But it's of use today.'

'Yes, I got him up a few days ago. He was not pleased. He won't like this, either.'

'Aye, once one has fairly gone into the grave, it'd be nice to expect a degree of peace to follow.'

'He's had plenty of *that*. The man's been dead for centuries. Here we are.' Theo held open the little iron-wrought gate for Ballantine, and followed him into the deserted churchyard. The hush, he reflected, might literally be termed deathly; a reflection which made him snicker, and wish that Gussie were about to hear the joke. She was sure to detest it.

He was agreeably surprised to find Lord Felix out of

107

his grave already, and sitting comfortably upon the headstone. His decayed head was turned up, his bony arms folded as he gazed at the distant stars.

'Fine night, isn't it?' said Theo, wandering up.

'What now do you want?' snapped Felix, without wresting his gaze from the firmament.

'I've got to go away for a spell, and I need you to watch the Book while I'm gone.'

'We are back to the singular, are we? Dare I hope it is because you've torn that dashed other Book to pieces?' His head came down; he caught sight of Ballantine's hulking shape, and nipped nimbly off his headstone at once, retreating to a distance of several feet. 'Come, come, boy, we can reach some agreement,' he said, scowling at the Runner. 'There's no need to beat me into it.'

'This is Mr. Ballantine, of the Bow Street Runners,' said Theo.

'And what are they?'

'Thief-takers, sir,' said Ballantine. 'Ordinarily, that is. I am of the Wyrde division.'

'So I perceive.'

Mr. Ballantine's tusks twitched. 'I'm here to take away that dashed other Book. I've begged your grandson's assistance.'

'Take it away to where?' said Lord Felix, but then he held up a hand. 'No, don't answer that. I do not care where you take it, provided that you *do*.'

'We are much obliged, sir,' said Mr. Ballantine.

Lord Felix looked at Theo, and his face developed a look of sudden cunning. 'Wait. Your father and mother are not yet returned, are they?'

'Not for a few days yet,' said Theo cautiously.

The disreputable old lord clapped his hands together, with enough force Theo half expected to see a finger fly off. 'Why, it's been a great many years since I last had sole charge of the Towers! What a happy idea! I'll do it.'

'They will be back soon,' Theo said. 'Expecting to find

the Towers still standing when they arrive.'

'Naturally.' Lord Felix beamed widely.

'I just mention the matter, in case you had any particularly outlandish notions in mind.'

The smile grew wider. 'Of course, my boy. Very sensible.'

Theo, afflicted with a feeling of impending doom, but unable to see any other way out of his predicament, achieved a sickly smile in return. 'Much obliged, sir.'

'You may bring me a good brandy, from wherever it is you are going.'

'Certainly.'

'A *good* brandy, mind. None of your cheap swill.'

Theo stared, fascinated by the vision of his undead lordship downing a bottle of Armagnac. 'You haven't any functional organs left, have you?' he suggested.

'What has that to do with anything?'

'Nothing.' Theo stepped back. 'We'll be off within an hour, I hope.'

Lord Felix dusted off his coat. 'Splendid. You may rely on me, my boy. I shall keep the place in excellent shape.'

Theo retreated, mentally washing his hands of the whole problem. If his parents were so unwise as to let Gussie talk them into going along with her hare-brained schemes, it was of no use blaming *him* when difficulties arose, and he was obliged to leave the Towers to the mercy of Lord Felix.

He returned into the house with Mr. Ballantine, pausing only to pen a missive to Lord and Lady Werth in explanation of his absence.

Then, leaving a servant to pack his valise, he returned downstairs.

Ballantine had brought the strong-box in, and set it at the top of the cellar stairs. The thing looked impenetrable: walls of steel an inch thick at least, with enough weight to counteract any antics of the curse-book, and with a tolerably fearsome-looking set of chains to wrap tight around it. Not to mention a lock as wide across as Ballantine's own ogrish hand.

'Will it do?' said the Runner.

'Let's hope so,' Theo said grimly.

TEN

The scene out at the family plot even took stout-hearted Gussie aback, so unusual a sight did it present.

A cluster of intrepid souls ventured out into the crisp, clear air, Gussie (thanks to Miss Frostell's efforts) closely wrapped up in her warmest pelisse, with a scarf about her neck. The two children of the house stuck close to them, Miss Selwyn claiming an incipient and paralysing boredom if she was left out of the scheme, and Lord Maundevyle venturing nothing in explanation of his curiosity save a slight smile.

Great-Aunt Honoria, of course, enjoyed the adventure to an uncommon degree. 'It's better than a picnic!' she declared, bobbing along above Gussie's head.

'With corpses in place of cake, and instead of porcelain tea-cups we shall have aged bones,' said Gussie. 'Nothing could be more delightful.'

'I knew you were a girl after my own heart,' said Great-Aunt Honoria.

The Selwyn family plot was attached to a tiny church situated on the border of the Starminster property. The church itself was in a state of disrepair: the begrimed glass panes of its arched windows sported more than one crack running through, and the grey stonework crumbled.

'What shocking neglect,' Gussie said, eyeing Lord Maundevyle with disapproval. 'Ought it not to be repaired?'

'It is not much used,' he excused himself. 'The parish is now served by a bigger, finer church a mile off.'

'Still, it is a charming old building, and deserves better treatment.'

'Then I shall attend to it directly,' Lord Maundevyle promised.

'Excellent,' said Gussie.

Miss Frostell intervened. 'My dear, his lordship may be safely left to the management of his own estates, mayn't he?'

'Oh, don't interfere!' begged Miss Selwyn. 'It pleases me no end to see Henry put in his place, and so neatly, too. I shall take notes.'

The whole party having, by this time, come upon the moss-grown collection of headstones making up the Selwyn family's resting place, conversation immediately died, for the full, magnificent panorama now became clear.

In the first place, there was Lord Werth, presiding over the unearthing of a grave in the centre of the churchyard. He had three gardeners under his direction, brawny young fellows with shovels; they were hard at work, and earth flew every which way. Several graves lay open to the air. Their occupants lounged about in postures of luxurious idleness, talking amongst themselves.

'Why, it *is* a picnic,' said Honoria in high glee, and swooped down upon them.

In the second instance, Lady Maundevyle had joined the venture. She and Lord Werth appeared to be getting along uncommonly well, to Gussie's amazed eye, and this despite the fact that her ladyship had not yet effected a full return to her usual form. Her legs might be restored to her, but her mouthful of sharp, bristling teeth flashed in the light as she laughed at some sally of my lord's.

And in the third place, dwarfing the proceedings with

her enormous bulk was Lady Margery, coiled in the frozen field adjacent to the churchyard, and resting her snout upon the ironwork fence. 'A little deeper, and you shall have him up!' she called encouragingly, blinking her great eyes. 'What shall this be, the fifth already? Prodigiously fine work!'

'Gracious,' said Gussie, picking her way carefully through the opened graves. 'My dear uncle, are you digging up every Selwyn in existence?'

A gleam of malevolent mischief appeared in my lord's eye. 'They are proving most conversable,' he assured his niece.

'Indeed, they are!' concurred her ladyship, with a trill of delighted amusement. 'I had no notion our forebears were such a witty lot.'

This prompted a ripple of laughter amongst the assembled corpses, and two or three bony elbows nudged their neighbours. 'Fine gal, ain't she?' said one of them.

'Doing the family proud,' agreed another.

Lady Maundevyle preened. 'Miss Werth, Henry, Clarissa. Will you permit me to introduce to you: Lord Maundevyle, Lord Maundevyle, Lord Edward, and Lady Maundevyle?' She pointed to each of the four unearthed corpses in turn, all of whom turned to stare with great curiosity at the newcomers.

'Werth,' said one. 'Daughter of yours, sir?'

'My niece,' said Lord Werth.

The decayed head nodded. Gussie beheld a grand, crumbling ruin of a man, clad in rotted scraps, with scarcely a shred of flesh left to him; nonetheless he contrived to muster nothing insignificant in the way of expression, and gave her a look that could politely be termed deeply appreciative. 'They always did make 'em bonny,' he said. 'Did not your nephew marry a Werth?' This being addressed to one of the others, Gussie couldn't tell which.

'No, that was Bella,' said one — the other Lady

Maundevyle?

'Fine, Wyrded stock,' said one of the Lord Maundevyles, grinning horribly with gumless teeth. 'You could do worse, grandson. Henry, was it?'

'It was, sir,' said the present Lord Maundevyle, and bowed.

The corpse nodded his head at Gussie. 'Fine girl. And she's brought her family, has she? Excellent. It's high time we strengthened our ties with other Wyrded families, and the Werths were always matchless in that.'

'If in nothing else,' Gussie murmured.

'Have I mentioned how obliged we are to Miss Werth?' said the living Lady Maundevyle, beaming her fish-smile at Gussie. 'It is to her capable assistance I owe my return to the Wyrde, and Henry also.'

'Goodness, but what a quantity of smiles,' Gussie said under her breath. 'I shall be having nightmares about them for weeks.'

'I'm afraid we mean to keep you,' said Miss Selwyn. 'You cannot get out of it now. They'll have your wedding to Henry planned by dinner time.'

Gussie made no immediate reply, being uncertain as to the state of her own feelings at such an idea. Her independence must rebel at the notion of her fate being so summarily decided, and by a pack of corpses besides. But the brief, sideways glance she directed at Henry revealed two things: the first being a profile she owned she found attractive, for he was a well-looking young man. The second being that the present Lord Maundevyle was looking sideways at her, too, and without any apparent feelings of horror. In fact, his dark grey eyes were merrily twinkling.

He spoke. 'It has to be said, nobody could bear with *this* abominable display so well as a Werth.'

'Which is fair and just, considering it is all my uncle's fault to begin with.'

'See,' said Miss Selwyn. 'It is destiny. Werths and

Selwyns, all Wyrded together.'

'Let the world tremble,' murmured Gussie.

Miss Selwyn smiled, almost as horribly as her mother. 'Oh, they will.'

Lady Maundevyle (the living one) did not appear to disapprove of her ancestors' plans either, judging from the complacent look she directed at Gussie and her son. Gussie recoiled from it, on account of there being a tinge of something else behind the smiling satisfaction.

'I believe your mama is planning something, and it isn't a wedding,' said Gussie. 'I would stake Great-Aunt Honoria's head on it. Is she not yet finished with me?'

'Not nearly,' said Miss Selwyn.

'But what further use could she find for poor, hapless me?'

'The family is bigger than just the four of us. There are cousins aplenty; some one or two aunts, and uncles; a quantity of second-cousins, and so on.'

'With whom to do what?' said Gussie dangerously. 'Must they all be Wyrded?'

'Oh, yes, *all*,' Miss Selwyn assured her. 'And after that, you must realise there is the rest of England.'

'The rest of England!'

'Beginning with those families enjoying a close alliance with ours, naturally.'

'I see,' said Gussie faintly.

'Mama envisions a return to the Wyrde en masse,' said Miss Selwyn kindly. 'It's her belief that anyone with the potential to turn Wyrded ought to do so. Then, you see, there could be no more talk of *licenses*, and *registration*, for there would be far too many of us. Indeed, perhaps the unWyrded may prove to be the minority.'

Gussie was silent, possibly with horror, possibly with awe.

'Mother does not shy away from a grand dream,' said the young Lord Maundevyle, with that ironic smile of his. 'It is best not to struggle too hard.'

'Says the man who hid from his mother for months together,' Gussie retorted.

'And I am grateful to your family for the reprieve.'

'You are very welcome, I'm sure.'

'But does it not occur to you that I may have had another motive for staying so long?'

'I am sure I cannot imagine what it might have been.' Gussie spoke the truth. To her mind, any outsider's voluntarily choosing to spend so many weeks together at the Towers, when the house was haunted by the likes of Great-Aunt Honoria and the grounds by Lord Felix, was incomprehensible. More likely that such a person sought refuge from a worse fate.

'Your aunt and uncle gave me to understand I might remain as long as I liked.'

'Did they though? How curious of them. We are not generally so welcoming.'

'The ritual proved otherwise, surely?'

'Not at all. You'll recall that most of the distant relations Lord Felix unearthed were sent packing in short order.'

'Well—'

'And most of them were glad to go, come to think of it. Why weren't *you*?'

Lord Maundevyle met her suspicious look with one of bland amusement. 'Come, are you not happy at the Towers?'

'Prodigiously, but as I seem to have said before lately, I was a Werth since birth. There was never any hope for *my* good sense.'

'Consider me an honorary Werth, then.'

'Impossible. You are far too sensible.'

'You seem to have received a curiously inaccurate impression of my character.'

'Well, you are so taciturn there is no making you out.'

Fittingly enough, Lord Maundevyle considered this sally in silence.

116

'And my point is made. Gentlemen!' Gussie clapped her hands, hoping to cut through the chatter prevailing between the unearthed Selwyns and the living ones. 'Ladies! If you would be so good as to give me your attention for a short time?'

Four withered heads turned in her direction — five, in fact, for Lord Werth's gardeners had succeeded in bringing up the fifth of Lady Maundevyle's dead relatives. Whoever it was levered him or herself out of the half-rotted coffin as Gussie spoke, and stood stretching luxuriously.

'My uncle had a purpose in waking you all up,' she continued. 'Did not you, sir? Shall you object to my laying it out?'

Lord Werth, fatigued by his efforts, leaned heavily against the nearest headstone, and waved a hand in Gussie's direction by way of assent.

'It is about a Book,' said Gussie. 'A very particular kind, not at all the sort to sit quietly upon a shelf but—'

'No!' cried the newly unearthed Selwyn in what seemed to Gussie a woman's voice. 'It is not returned? How can that be?'

'No, no,' Gussie said, as soothingly as she could. 'If you refer to your own family's specimen then I know nothing of its whereabouts. That is exactly what I wished to ask *you*.'

'Calm yourself, Lady Muriel,' said Lady Maundevyle (the living one) in a ringing tone. 'Such discomposure is not seemly.'

Lady Muriel stiffened. '*Seemly?*' she spat. 'It is not *seemly* what that Book did to our family! And the way Osbert coddled it, and defended it, though it would have murdered us all in our beds! Hah! He paid for it in the end, did not he?'

'Osbert,' said Gussie sharply. 'Is he the one in the painting?'

She did not, as it turned out, need to explain which painting she meant. 'Lord Maundevyle as was,' said Lady

Muriel, nodding, and added with venom, 'A prize fool.'

'Can I talk to him?' Gussie undertook a quick survey of the remaining, untouched graves. 'Is he here?'

'I should think it unlikely,' said Lady Muriel with a sniff. 'He was burned.'

'Burned? By the Book?'

'Not *seemly*, was it?' she said, with a snide look at a deeply offended Lady Maundevyle.

But that great lady would not be cowed by a corpse. 'That must have been long ago,' said she with unimpaired dignity. 'We have known nothing of such improper pursuits in *my* day.'

'That is because I and my sister Gundred made away with it.' Lady Muriel's death's head stretched in a hollow smile. 'How it screamed,' she said, dreamily.

'We are all very grateful, I am sure,' said Lady Maundevyle stiffly.

'No we are not!' said Clarissa. 'You cannot think how *dull* it has been all this while. Not the smallest excitement to be had anywhere — not one singular event, or peculiar happenstance! — and when *finally* something of note takes place at Starminster we owe it to a Werth!' She folded her arms, and glared at Lady Muriel.

'You had rather be hacked to pieces by a Book than suffer a degree of boredom, had you?' said Muriel, dripping sarcasm.

'Yes,' said Clarissa.

One of the dead Lord Maundevyles gave a crack of laughter. 'One of your lot, Ned, I reckon!' he said.

Ned, or Lord Edward, snickered, and offered Clarissa a salute. 'Am I to hope your elder brother takes after me as well?'

'Not in the least, sir,' said Lord Maundevyle. 'I like a quiet life.'

Lord Edward, crushed with disappointment, turned away.

'And yet *you* have seen fit to abandon us for the Towers

all this while,' said Clarissa, turning a still livid countenance upon her brother. 'And goodness knows where Charles has gone!'

'It was ungenerous of us to leave you here alone,' he allowed.

'She was not alone,' said Lady Maundevyle with strong displeasure. 'She had *me*.'

'As I said,' murmured Lord Maundevyle. 'Ungenerous.'

'Anyway,' Gussie intervened. 'If any of you might happen to remember where the Book came from that killed Lord Osbert, we shall be most interested to hear of it.'

'Why do you ask?' said Lady Muriel.

'Because we have got one of our own, and lately it has tried to kill me.'

Lady Muriel flung up her hands in disbelief, and walked over to the iron-wrought fence. She leaned upon it, not far from where Lady Margery lay, and stood shaking her head. 'Not a scrap of sense among them,' she informed the dragon.

Lady Margery nodded her great head in commiseration. 'I *tried*,' she said. 'Dragon-fire would do for it, no doubt about that. But would they let me? No!'

Lady Muriel lapsed into a brooding silence.

'Anyone?' Gussie said, surveying the row of grave-begrimed lords and ladies with flagging hopes.

'Before our time, I think?' said one of the Lord Maundevyles.

'Never heard of it before today,' said Lord Edward affably. 'Wish I had, though. What a lark!'

This remark sent Lady Muriel into a fresh round of vituperation, most of which was uttered at too low a volume to reach Gussie's ears.

At length she stalked back towards the opened graves, and got straight into hers. 'The Book,' she said awfully, 'was given to House Maundevyle in the year 1482. It was a gift.'

Gussie straightened, electrified. 'A gift! From whom?'

Lady Muriel looked Gussie squarely in the eye. 'From *your* family,' she said, and fell back into her grave with a *thump* and a cloud of loose earth.

Lady Margery reared up, hissing. '*Our* family! No! That is not possible.'

Gussie, shocked speechless, could only blink.

'Goodness me,' said Clarissa into the ensuing silence. 'You do seem to be rather a disastrous lot, don't you?'

ELEVEN

The "conveyance", as Ballantine termed it, scarcely deserved the name. Theo concluded this, with some bitterness, after an uncountable number of hours on the road between the Towers and London.

Never had ninety miles seemed longer.

Already covering no inconsiderable distance, the journey was lengthened (in seeming, if not in reality) by the state of the roads (execrable); by the utter lack of even basic comforts afforded by the squarish box-on-wheels Ballantine pleased to call a coach; and by the behaviour of the curse-book, which chose to imagine itself put-upon.

'We *have* abducted it, in a literal sense,' Ballantine said, an hour or so into the nightmarish journey. 'We asked no permission, handled it most urgently, and now refuse to grant it its liberty. I think you and I would feel some indignation ourselves, were we to be treated so.'

The Runner had not, after all, returned to the less alarming of his two forms. Theo perfectly understood, and supported, his reasons; given the choice, he would rather have an ogre along for this little errand than a mere man. Nonetheless, Ballantine's great, hulking bulk opposite him inside the unlovely conveyance only served to remind him of the fraught nature of their mission. They needed *muscle*.

Theo made some ungracious response to this attempt to win sympathy for the book.

'I thought to appeal to your better feelings,' said Ballantine, with a smile in his voice, and even in the deep dark of the moonless night Theo saw the tusks either side of his mouth move.

'When you have known me for a little longer, you will understand that I have no better feelings,' said Theo.

'But that can't be true, can it? After all, here you are.'

'Lack of choice.'

'Not to a man with no better feelings. You could have hurled me out into the snow, and thrown the curse-book after me.'

Theo was silent, occupied with a sense of bitter regret that this option had not occurred to him at the time.

'No, you wouldn't have done it,' said Ballantine. 'Even if you had thought of it, which I suspect you did not.'

'And are you a reader of minds, as well as an ogre?' growled Theo, none too pleased at this series of too-accurate reflections.

'No. But I do flatter myself I've a way of getting a man's measure.'

'Woman's, too, or does the fairer sex elude you?'

'Woman's as well. Take Lady Werth, for example. Probably the most good-hearted of the lot of you, if a trifle placid — except when she's angered or afraid, and then she's a different woman altogether.'

Theo inclined his head. The portrait of his mother was not inaccurate.

'And Miss Werth. She would have us all believe she has no heart at all, but—'

'No, that is actually true,' Theo put in.

Ballantine chuckled. 'Perhaps it is,' he allowed, and Theo could not tell if he meant it or not.

The conversation here lapsed, for the curse-book saw an opportunity to cause a ruckus, and took it with gusto. Theo sat holding one side of the strong-box in a white-knuckled grip, while Ballantine's still stronger hands steadied the other. They hung on in grim silence as the box rocked wildly back and forth, and ignored as best they could the inarticulate screaming sound that came from within.

'Lady Honoria interests me perhaps the most,' said Ballantine, when the curse-book fell silent. 'I would give a deal to know whether she was always as she is now, even when she was alive.'

'Better question,' said Theo, cautiously relaxing his hold on the strong-box. 'Was she ever alive?'

'Surely she must have been?'

'For her first three years, perhaps,' Theo said. 'Might have turned revenant on her birthday.'

'You don't know for certain?'

'I don't believe anyone has ever asked.'

'That would make more sense than not,' mused Ballantine. 'Hers is a personality I make no apology in terming freakish. She talks, and acts, as a woman without human qualities at all.'

'Bad influence on Gussie,' said Theo. 'I've always thought it.'

'And you are a good one?'

'Oh, no,' said Theo. 'But then, I spend little time at the cottage. Aunt Honoria is always going out there.'

'They do seem to get along well.'

'You've paid attention, haven't you? I did not think you had spent time enough at the Towers to notice so much.'

'I am interested in people,' said Ballantine. 'And your family is more interesting than most.'

'To say the least,' muttered Theo.

The journey went on in like fashion: conversation with Ballantine on any of a variety of subjects, interspersed with intervals of silence, and periodic struggles with the curse-book. They were not more than halfway to London before Theo felt a mass of bruises, jolted as he was in the poorly sprung coach, and half frozen besides.

Ballantine bore it all without complaint; indeed, without uttering so much as a single curse. He had already declared that he bore with the winter cold better as an ogre — scarcely seemed to feel it, in fact — but he behaved as though he felt none of the bumps and bounces either, and Theo felt a growing envy of the man's Wyrde. Ugly he was, but what of that? To a man who cared nothing for his appearance (such as Theo), an ogre's shape had many an advantage.

These reflections leading him inevitably to the subject of his own Wyrde, and its various drawbacks, he became aware of a gnawing hunger, masked somewhat by the greater discomforts of the road.

'I ought to eat,' he said, an hour or so later, with the night going on forever all around him, and no prospect of stopping for food or rest until London was reached. 'We are in a fair woodland, I believe. I ought to be able to catch something suitable.'

'I had rather not stop,' said Ballantine, 'if you can hold your hunger until London.'

'I can,' said Theo. 'But I had much rather not. Come, I will catch enough for two.'

A moment's silence. 'What are you catching?' said the Runner.

'A rabbit, by preference, or some such thing.'

'I do like rabbit,' Ballantine allowed. 'Baked in a pie, with gravy—'

'No!' Theo said, revolted. 'Raw and fresh, and oozing blood.'

Ballantine sighed. 'The worst of it is, *both* sound appealing to me, at least in this state.'

'Good God, man, think what you are saying! What could be better? The best of both worlds is yours.'

'I will wait with the box,' said Ballantine. 'It's been quiet a while, but I'd urge you to hurry.'

Theo made no answer to this save a terse nod, which the Runner in all likelihood had not the eyes to detect, and threw open the coach door. He sank half up to his ankles in sodden snow, and briefly regretted that the dictates of his stomach had overpowered his sense.

But the ogre behind him would never be daunted by such a trifle, so Theo swallowed his distaste, and strode off into the dark depths of the silent wood.

He had a way of moving in near silence, despite the brittle twigs and branches littering the woodland floor, and all covered in snow. Even he could not have said whether this, too, was a product of his Wyrde, or whether the consequence of necessity, and long practice. Either way, he stalked the night-dark woods with a predator's stealth, and returned to the coach replete, and without having been gone for more than half an hour. In each hand he held an offering for the ogrish Runner, damn him.

He opened the coach door with due caution, alert for signs or sounds of trouble. None came. He climbed in, shaking the slush of half-melted snow off the hem of his heavy great-coat, and sat down in his former seat, careful to navigate around the centre of the floor, where the strong-box sat.

'I have procured two,' said he, and held them out.

No reply came.

So intent had Theo been upon the feast he held in his hands, and the problem of the curse-book — it would not do to drop the former, or disturb the latter — only now did it occur to him that something was missing from the coach.

In fact, everything was missing from the coach. The opposite seat sat empty, and the space where the strong-box had been was empty too.

Theo sat in frozen, horrified silence for an instant only. Then he was out of the coach again, heedless of the deep snow, and roaring Ballantine's name into the still, uncaring air.

No answer came. Snarling curses, he went around the coach to where Ballantine's coachman sat, picking his way around the four sturdy horses, whose tranquillity might reassure him were the situation not so damned strange. 'You there!' he called. 'Where's your master?'

'What, ain't he in the coach, sir?'

'No! Nor is the damned box.'

The coachman clambered down, verified the truth of Theo's words with a survey of the coach's interior, and stood scratching his head. 'If anybody could walk off wi' the box it'd be Mr. Ballantine,' he offered.

'I am well aware that he has more than might enough to manage such an article,' Theo said with rising irritation. 'What I am less certain of is *why* he would do so. Especially having requested *my* aid, on account of being unable—' He stopped in the middle of this promising rant, some peculiarity among the surrounding snow having caught his eye. He travelled a few steps, stooped, and undertook a close scrutiny of the ground.

'Look,' he said sharply, and pointed. 'Look there. What do you see?'

The coachman, an obliging soul if not especially blessed with wit, bent down. 'Not much,' he admitted. 'Happen it's too dark.'

'What you *see*,' said Theo, 'or *would* see if you had not such useless eyes, is too many footprints.'

'Too many, my lord?'

'You see my footprints, and your own. A great, oversized set which I take to be Ballantine's. And then marks indicating the passage of three other feet.'

'Three?' The coachman directed at Theo a look of befuddled enquiry.

'It is perfectly clear what's happened,' said Theo.

'Is it, sir?'

'*Yes.* Where do you suppose these three feet came from, my good man?'

'I couldn't say, sir.'

'What being anywhere near, or indeed *in*, this detestable equipage could possibly possess exactly three feet? Not

126

two, and not four, but *three*.' Theo tore at his hair in pure frustration, and indulged himself further in stamping about in a circle. 'The blessed *book*!' he shouted. 'Or perhaps more rightly, the box we put the thrice-cursed thing *in*!'

'You mean to say, sir, that—'

'That the damned and double-damned Book has caused its prison *to grow legs,* and the whole damned lot has walked away! See! They are not human feet, my dear fellow, are they?' He pointed again at a neat, clear cluster of them etched deeply into the snow — doubtless marking where the strong-box had, under the Book's direction, jumped down from the coach, immediately prior to running away. 'I might say they belonged to a cat of some sort, save that they are much too big, and this is not the region for such great felines as that. All of that quite apart from the fact that there are only *three of them!* Why three, I ask you? Why? If it must grow legs and run off, why would not it produce something sensible, like four?'

Theo, aware that anger, frustration and alarm were turning him a trifle overwrought, took a deep gulping breath, and endeavoured to progress to the state of icy, calm anger he much preferred. It helped, a little.

'You going after them, sir?' said the coachman.

'On that point I am undecided,' he said. 'If the strong-box has run away, then certainly Ballantine has gone after it, and may be in need of aid. On the other hand, he may have managed the matter already, in which case to go haring off into the trees after him would only place *two* of us at an inconvenient distance from the coach, and complicate everything horribly.' Even as he spoke, his brain reeled under the picture now presented to it. Legs. The Books could grow *legs.*

His brain, though, was of the first-class sort that could not long dither in indecision, even having suffered a shock. He gave a growling sigh, mustered himself for another dive into the cold, and took off at a run. 'I'll return shortly!' he called over his shoulder to the abandoned coachman.

'Hold the coach there!'

The Book, whether by happenstance or cunning design (Theo would have put money on the latter), had hurtled off in the opposite direction from the one Theo himself had previously taken. Accordingly, nothing of the escape, or its pursuit, had reached his ears; the dulcet woodlands had seemed to him an oasis of wintry peace.

Not now. He had not followed the trail very far before he began to hear signs of some altercation raging not far away. Ballantine's light Scottish burr became discernible soon afterwards, though there was nothing of the ear-splitting scream that the Books were capable of mustering when they chose. Instead he heard that repulsive whispering again, together with a horrible snarling and muttering.

He came upon them to find Ballantine had prevailed (to his secret relief). The ogre sat upon the weathered stump of a fallen old oak, catching his breath. Before him writhed the strong-box, fallen on its side in the snow. Its three legs, their shape borrowed indeed from some feline idea (and to Theo's mind, unquestionably demonic in nature), were trussed up tightly together, and consequently it could not move.

'Why, they even have fur,' said Theo as he drew level with Ballantine. 'The attention to detail is truly remarkable.'

Fascination had overtaken alarm in his scholar's brain, at least once the worst outcomes of the night's adventure had proved averted. But his apparent insouciance irritated the Runner, for he said, with unwonted irony, 'No need to worry, my lord, for as you can see I am perfectly *fine*.'

'I told you, I have no better feelings,' said Theo, crouching down beside the felled strong-box.

'Did you know it could do this?'

'The legs? Not a notion.'

'Did *any* of you know?'

128

'Have to ask my father,' said Theo, poking one of the legs, which promptly kicked him. 'Ouch. But I think not.'

'Fascinating.'

'But then, none of us has ever locked the things in boxes and made off with them, either. Nor been so unwise as to spend more than a few minutes in the same room with either of them. For all I know, they might grow legs every night, and run around their cells like chickens.'

Ballantine's silence was of a resentful quality.

'Though I should think it unlikely. I go in from time to time unannounced, and I never saw any legs on them before.' He took hold of one of the feet, in a more powerful grip, and examined it as closely as he dared. 'Five toes to each,' he reported. 'Grey-furred. Claws are longer and thicker than might be expected, and quite black.' He performed a speedy count, just in case he had, in his haste, mistaken the evidence of his eyes; but no. Three there were. 'Why *three*?' he asked of no one in particular. 'That's the part I do not understand.'

'*That* is the part you don't understand?' Ballantine bellowed. Theo heard bones crack as the huge ogre flexed some unpromisingly muscled section of his anatomy.

'If you are going to fell anybody with what is no doubt a punishing right,' said Theo, 'I beg you to exercise your ire upon the Book, or perhaps the strong-box, rather than upon me.'

'Not the box,' snarled Ballantine. 'Maybe the Book, though.'

'I wonder where it was going?' Theo mused.

'Anywhere but Bow Street, at any rate.' Ballantine gave a sigh; his rage seemed all gone. 'Truth to tell, if I had known it had this capability I'd not have suggested this journey.'

'But then we would not have learned anything new about it,' said Theo, straightening. 'And is not *that* the ultimate goal, after all?'

'Provided it doesn't include the thing's getting away

from us, and terrorising the good people of — of wherever we are.' Ballantine cast a useless look around, as though some quality of the silhouetted oaks and elms around him might answer this question, and abandoned the subject with a shrug. 'Let's get it back to the coach, if we can.'

'Now that it's trussed, there should be no difficulty,' said Theo, with an optimism even he found foolhardy. 'How did you manage that, by the by?'

Ballantine patted his pockets. 'It is not quite the first time I've had to apprehend a fleeing miscreant.'

'No doubt you have all manner of fearsome kit in there. Can you carry this particular miscreant? I shall play guard.'

Ballantine bent down, grasped the steel box, and lifted it with enviable ease. The legs kicked uselessly. 'What say you to no more stops, now, till London?'

'No more stops,' Theo agreed. 'You'll find dinner waiting in the coach, however.'

Ballantine brightened. 'Happen you're a useful fellow to have along after all.'

'Much obliged.'

TWELVE

Lady Muriel Selwyn's revelation dictated the prevailing subject of conversation at Starminster for two days together. By the end of this period, Gussie would cheerfully have throttled every one of her companions if it was the only way to make them stop.

'But *why* would your dear family have done anything so wicked?' repeatedly protested Miss Frostell, much more cast down by the idea than Gussie, or for that matter, Lord Werth.

'Sabotage!' proclaimed Clarissa, gesturing extravagantly. 'Here are we, eager to clasp these excellent Werths to our bosoms, and all the while they have been plotting against us!'

'Yes, and on account of our being filthy betrayers we must instantly leave Starminster,' said Gussie.

'No!' Clarissa took hold of Gussie's arm, and bodily prevented her from doing any such thing. 'You cannot! Not when things are finally getting *good*.'

'It is regrettable,' was Lord Werth's judgement of the situation.

'I am sure your noble ancestors had no idea of the Book's causing us the least harm,' said Lady Maundevyle several times over, all graciousness.

Lady Werth, a persistent frown indicating a troubled mind, only repeated a few platitudes. As for Great-Aunt Honoria, she held forth for the rest of the day, and well into the next, with several possible explanations drawn from her own nightmare of a mind, each more lurid than the last.

Only Lady Margery continued untouched by the news, once she had recovered from the initial shock. 'It can only be the most scandalous falsehood,' she said firmly, and ordered another two bowls of crème anglaise.

This fever of speculation and protest was interrupted at last by the arrival of a letter from the Towers. Nothing in *that* to cause any alarm, Gussie would have said — unless any could attach to the unusual circumstance of Theo's having actually written to his parents.

Except that it did. She read disquiet in her uncle's tight-lipped silence as he handed the letter to his wife, having perused it over his empty breakfast-plate.

Lady Werth read it quickly through, and gave a gasp. Gussie was further interested to see the beginnings of ice-crystals forming in her hair, all at once, indicating that her aunt was in the grip of some strong, and negative, emotion.

'How could he be so *foolish*?' she said in a sudden burst of anger, her gaze seeking out her husband's for reassurance.

'I am sure it seemed best to Theo, my dear,' said Lord Werth, though in a tone suggestive of no such serenity as he affected. 'And it would indeed be a relief to be rid of one of the Books.'

Gussie looked her enquiry.

'Oh, you had better read it,' said Lady Werth, and handed the letter to Gussie.

Having done so, Gussie, unwisely, laughed.

'It is no laughing matter!' said Lady Werth, rising from the breakfast-table, and making a distracted bow in Lady

Maundevyle's direction. 'Forgive us, Esther, but we must take our leave today.'

'Nothing *bad* has happened, has it?' said Clarissa eagerly, leaning forward.

'Not yet,' said Lady Werth, and swept out of the room.

'Lord Bedgberry has gone away from home on an errand of some urgency,' said Gussie.

'How unfortunate,' said Lady Maundevyle. 'I hope nothing too disastrous?'

'Bound to be,' Gussie said cheerfully. 'He has taken one of the Books out of the cellar, which can only go horribly wrong, and he has left a corpse in charge of the Towers. All perfectly reasonable to Theo, I dare say.'

'Perfectly, perfectly,' said Great-Aunt Honoria.

'Nothing in any of *that* to alarm my poor aunt, but she is given to these occasional bursts of irrationality.'

'A corpse,' repeated Clarissa slowly. 'How original.'

'Yes, isn't it? I had better go and pack.'

Which she did forthwith, but as she descended the stairs again, the better part of an hour later, she found Lady Maundevyle waiting at the bottom of them.

It being possible that my lady lay in wait for someone else altogether, Gussie attempted to sweep past, with only a polite nod in her ladyship's direction.

But it was not to be. 'Miss Werth,' said the lady, moving to intercept. 'I must speak to you.'

'Good gracious, what can possibly be so serious?' said Gussie, for Lady Maundevyle wore an expression of portentous gravity, and comported herself with a decided air of importance.

'It is a situation of the most severe,' she said. 'Miss Werth, words can never express my gratitude to you for your service to my family. Never again will we be so diminished, so *unworthy*. Any service I, or my family, can hitherto perform for your benefit shall be done in an instant. You have only to ask.'

'Thank you,' said Gussie, frowning, for she anticipated

yet more. 'But?'

Lady Maundevyle frowned, too.

'There is a "but" on its way, is not there?' Gussie prompted. 'You have already thanked me. You were not lying in wait down here purely in order to do so again.'

'No. There is yet more I would ask of you.'

Gussie gave a small, half-smothered sigh.

'Though it is not rightly *I* who asks it of you, Miss Werth. One might more rightly say, the world demands it of you!'

Gussie, distracted by the reflection that Clarissa would be a perfect copy of her mother in another twenty years, made no reply.

'Can you doubt what it is I am going to say?'

'In point of fact, I wish you would say it at once. I believe my aunt and uncle would like to be gone within the half-hour.' She had not forgotten Clarissa's prediction as to her ladyship's latest inspired plan, but harboured some small hopes that the younger lady might have been mistaken.

'Get out into the world, Miss Werth,' said she. 'Mix with as many people as you can. *Wyrde* as many people as you can. History has not always been kind to those touched by the Wyrde, has it? The future may be less so, *if* we do not act. And you, with your wonderful Wyrde, *you* can change everything.'

'This is about the registration scheme, is it?' said Gussie. 'You cannot think the government will abandon such plans merely because there are more of us. They are much more likely to be more committed to the idea than ever, especially if many of these new Wyrded souls should prove of the dangerous sort.'

'That may be so,' allowed her ladyship. 'But—'

'And the moment it becomes known that I am waltzing about the country, making wyverns and mermaids and gorgons out of half the people I meet, I shall find myself locked up upon the instant.'

'There is power in numbers, Miss Werth; none at all in isolation.'

'Now I perceive! A cunning scheme of revenge, to be sure. If my ancestors were so disobliging as to saddle yours with one of *those* Books, you shall contrive to have their unlucky descendants taken up as criminals. We shall be amply repaid. All things considered, it is only fair.'

Lady Maundevyle afforded this sally only the faintest of smiles. 'You must try, Miss Werth.'

'No. No, I really must not. If I were to so much as propose the idea, my aunt would lock me up herself — and I do not even think she would be wrong to do so.'

Lady Maundevyle said nothing more, but favoured Gussie with a speaking look expressive of a boundless disappointment.

'If you will excuse me,' said Gussie, curtseying, 'I believe we have a situation to manage at home. Please accept my grateful thanks for your hospitality.'

'And I do not even know why we have rushed about in all this hurry, for there is no possibility we can arrive in time to prevent some disaster,' said Lady Werth, a half-hour or so later, the Werths having been ruthlessly packed into their travelling-coach and sent hurtling on their way back into Norfolk. 'Lord Felix will have pulled the Towers down around his grubby ears before we have covered half the distance.'

'He shall do nothing of the sort,' said Lord Werth, clasping his wife's hand in a soothing grip. 'He reigned over the Towers for some years when he was alive, and the building stands yet.'

'He had not then suffered centuries of boredom as a corpse,' her ladyship retorted.

'A fair argument,' Gussie murmured. 'If I had lain in a grave for a hundred years, I should like above anything to pull down a house or two upon my awakening. I cannot think of a single more enlivening way to celebrate.'

'I expect to find not a drop of brandy left in the house,' Lord Werth allowed. 'And considerable inroads made upon my wine cellar, too. But beyond that I shouldn't think we have much to fear from Lord Felix.'

Gussie found herself in agreement with her aunt, though without the more exaggerated of her imaginings. Lord Felix unleashed! There was a terrible prospect. In her view, he would use the time to resurrect the Towers he had known in his youth; but what that would consist of, she struggled to predict.

That it might involve unwise use of the Book, that was a distinct possibility. Lord Felix had sent them to consult the thing over the Assembly. He had then gone ahead and performed the summoning, despite myriad perfectly sensible reasons not to do so. What else might he dredge up out of the Book's miserable depths, given unrestrained access to it for days together? And what might he do with them?

These were weighty reflections, but unlike Lady Werth, Gussie found that curiosity won out over apprehension. Lord Felix might be trouble, but his disregard for due caution had had its benefits before. He would make a deal of a mess, but he would emerge enlightened on all sorts of points that it had never occurred to Gussie to investigate.

All things considered, she was rather looking forward to getting home.

This comfortable state persisted all the way across the country, despite her aunt's frosty state, and Great-Aunt Honoria's gleefully disastrous predictions. It persisted even as the coach drew up the driveway and stopped in front of the Towers' front doors — which, oddly, hung open.

'Ah, we are on fire,' said Gussie as she stepped down, the acrid smell of smoke near overwhelming her the moment her head emerged from the coach. 'Excellent. It is a positive *age* since we last had a good burning.'

'I wonder who is being burned?' said Lord Werth

mildly, handing his wife down from the coach.

'Who?' Gussie repeated, briefly nonplussed. 'I had imagined only a *what*, but I'm sure you have it right, uncle.'

Lord Werth drew in a great breath of smoky air, and to Gussie's fascination, smiled. 'I hope it is not Silvester,' he commented, and withdrew into the house.

Lady Werth closed her eyes in momentary despair. '*Someone* is shortly to be burned,' she said ominously. 'And if his name is not Felix, I shall eat my gloves.'

'We shall ask Mrs. Gosling's assistance,' said Gussie, taking her aunt's arm. 'The application of a little sauce would make a glove or two much more palatable.'

'That won't be necessary,' said Lady Werth. 'I shall myself preside over the burning of Lord Felix.'

Gussie patted her arm. 'And he will scream horribly,' she said in a soothing way.

Inside, all appeared to be in order. No raging fires met Lady Werth's apprehensive eye. No mutilated corpses lay sprawled in doorways, nor were there signs that anything decomposing — or betentacled — had lately run amok. To be sure, some few articles of furniture or ornament had been moved about, and put in odd places, but that was all.

Considering the heavy aroma of smoke upon the air, the effect was more unnerving than otherwise.

'Felix!' called Lord Werth. 'Where the devil are you?'

There came a shambling step, and Lord Felix promptly appeared in a far doorway. He had come from a period of high revel, Gussie judged, for the reek of spirits emanating from the old lord almost outdid the stench of smoke. 'I don't ordinarily care for cognac overmuch,' he said, with a wide smile. 'But this is not bad, sir. Not bad at all.' He saluted Lord Werth with a half-empty glass, and drank heavily.

'Felix!' proclaimed Lady Werth in ringing tones. 'What have you done to our home?'

'Rearranged it a bit,' said Lord Felix, gesturing with his empty glass. 'We had better notions as to the arranging of

137

things, in my day. Got the footmen to do it.'

'My concerns as to the placements of my tapestries cannot *quite* equal my concerns as to the state of your fires,' retorted she.

'Fires?' said Lord Felix, and looked about the hall, as though he might catch a glimpse of some overlooked blaze. 'What?'

'The air is thick with smoke!'

'Oh, that.' Felix studied the inside of his glass, frowning. 'That's the Book. Have you got any more of the cognac?'

'The Book! You haven't burned it?' Lady Werth's face turned ice-white in a sadly literal sense, and Gussie hastened to intervene.

'Better if he has,' she reminded her aunt. 'The thing's trouble.'

'But our *history*—'

'Not worth our lives, surely?'

Lady Werth took a few rapid breaths. 'Ancestors witness, I will burn him alive and *screaming*—'

'Haven't been alive in many a year,' said Lord Felix, affably untouched by this threat. 'Dare say I could achieve a tolerable scream, however, under the right circumstances.'

Lord Werth held up a hand. 'Let us establish the facts. Have you burned the Book of Werth, my lord?'

'As a matter of fact, I haven't.'

'Something else?'

Lord Felix shook his head. 'Splendid notion, however. Wish I had thought of it.'

'Where, then, is the smoke coming from?'

Lord Felix's sigh indicated a vast exasperation. 'As I have *told* you, it's the Book.'

'The Book is... smoking?'

The extent of the old lord's mirth no doubt attributable to his inebriated state. He bent double in paroxysms of laughter, the brandy glass falling from

138

shaking fingers. 'Smoking! A fine tobacco, no doubt.'

'At this point,' said Lord Werth, 'there is very little of which I wouldn't imagine that Book capable.'

'Well, and perhaps it is, at that,' said Lord Felix, still cackling. 'Point of fact, it's been throwing out smoke since this morning.'

'And why would it do that?'

'Excellent question. Yesterday it flooded the cellar, and the day before...' Lord Felix paused to wrack what was left of his brains. 'Ah yes. Day before was the blood.'

'*Blood?*' fairly shrieked Lady Werth. 'Whose blood?'

'Not mine, at any rate. Shouldn't think I had any left.'

'Felix—'

'Maybe the servants.' Lord Felix shrugged his bony shoulders. 'Painted it all up and down the walls. Passingly artistic, I thought.'

'And the source of all this poor behaviour is...?' prompted Lord Werth.

'If you mean *I* have done something to it, I resent that,' said Lord Felix. 'Any further such aspersions will be met with the utmost indignation.' His eyes glinted. 'I should urge you to name your friends, sir.'

'No, you will not call me out over an insult I have not even uttered,' said Lord Werth.

Lord Felix's lip curled. 'Lily-liver,' he pronounced.

'Is it true that the curse-book is gone?' put in Gussie.

'It is! Behold me celebratory,' said the old lord, scrambling to retrieve his discarded glass. He toasted Gussie with this, winked, and downed contents which must, at this point, be purely imaginary.

'I should think it's sulking, then,' she suggested. 'This recalcitrance is a form of protest.'

'Am I to understand my son has not yet returned?' said Lady Werth.

'Cannot say as I have seen him,' said Lord Felix.

Lady Werth put her hands to her bonnet, a gesture of helpless despair. The frost had largely gone from her face again, however, so Gussie was in no immediate expectation of having an ice-statue on her hands. 'I shall oversee the unpacking,' she said, with a dark look at Lord Felix, and swept out.

Lord Werth plucked the glass from his ancestor's hand, and set it down upon a nearby table with a *thunk*. 'Come with me,' he ordered. 'This smoke will not do at all.'

'What do you imagine *I* am going to do about it?'

'One way or another, *we* are going to subdue the Book,' said Lord Werth grimly, and strode out of the hall.

Gussie exchanged a look with Miss Frostell.

Miss Frostell sneezed.

'Come, let us get you out of the way,' Gussie said, leading her companion back to the door. 'Jem Coachman will deliver you to the cottage, which, I trust, is smoke-free.'

'Oh, no,' protested Miss Frostell. 'I must stay and assist.'

'How exactly?'

'Well—'

'You are tired, poor Frosty, and I should think you are ravenously hungry besides. I know *I* am. I will join you shortly for a mighty dinner, you may be sure.'

'But what are you going to do?'

'Nothing of which you would not approve, I assure you,' said Gussie, perhaps mendaciously, though when roused to enthusiasm there was not much in which the obliging Miss Frostell would not join her erstwhile charge.

Having successfully ushered her biddable governess back into the coach, and seen her on her way to peace and comfort, Gussie thought herself at liberty to return inside — and made her way instantly down into the cellar.

The smoke was a great deal thicker below, and Gussie paused to wrap a length of her shawl over her face. Little light illuminated the worn old stairs, and she was forced to go slowly, with one hand held to the wall to steady herself. At length she reached the bottom, and made her way to the door of the Book's prison.

The door stood open.

Gussie froze. For a long moment she stood motionless, not even breathing, paralysed with horror (and, if we are to be honest, an unseemly degree of excitement). She listened hard for any sound of impending disaster; a scuttling of many appendages, say, as death scurried across the floor towards her. Or a distant scream of terror, as the Book savaged some other, more unfortunate soul.

'Uncle?' she called at last, when nothing but a heavy silence met her ears. 'Lord Felix?'

She thought she heard footfalls some little distance away, rather deeper into the cellar. Steeling herself — for if she was to die at any moment, it would not do for her corpse to be discovered with an expression of witless terror melded into its dead features — she ventured in the direction of the sounds. Her progress was slower than ever, for they had used up the day in travelling; late afternoon afforded only a dim glimmer of light, and Gussie walked mostly in shadow.

So dark was it, she almost fell over the prone form of Lord Felix before her eyes perceived him. He lay in a graceless heap upon the damp stone, limbs akimbo.

Her first thought was that he was dead, an idea she experienced with an agreeable thrill of horror. Then, recollecting that death had yet to do more than slow the old lord down (and only then, a very little), she bent down, and peered into his face. 'Sir?' she said. 'What has happened?'

He scowled up at her, and writhed upon the floor in the oddest fashion. 'Damned thing's broken my leg,' he grumbled.

'If that's so, you had better lie still,' she said. 'You will only make it worse, gyrating about like that.'

Lord Felix subsided, and lay like the corpse he was. 'Your uncle has it,' he said moodily. 'Yonder.' And he nodded his head in the direction of an arched doorway

141

some several feet distant.

'Wait here,' said Gussie unnecessarily, and trotted after her uncle.

She found him occupying the very centre of a room well stocked with wine. Racks filled with corked bottles lined the walls, thick with dust in many parts, though not all; the present Lord Werth's taste for wine could not equal his predecessor's, but nor did it fall far short. He stood in an attitude of high alertness, head raised, obviously listening.

'Uncle—' whispered Gussie.

He held a finger to his lips, an order Gussie obeyed. He followed this with an irritated, get-thee-gone gesture in the direction of the doorway, an order which Gussie had no intention whatsoever of following.

Her eyes scanned the cellar-room, to little effect. Only the foremost ranks of bottles could be discerned; the rest were swathed in shadow.

The Book, she gathered, lurked somewhere within.

Or — not. Movement stirred to her left; her quick eyes caught a glimpse of worn old leather; she pounced.

'I have it!' she called, wrapping both hands tightly around the fleeing Book, and hugging it close to her torso.

'Good God, Gussie, did I not tell you to *go*?' snapped Lord Werth, by her side in an instant. He took the Book from her. 'Go! I shall have everything secure in a moment.'

But the Book did not consent to be parted from Gussie. For barely five seconds had she held the Book in her arms; more than sufficient time, it proved, for it to return her clinging embrace. Several appendages had got around her, and clung tight.

'Why, I think it likes me,' said Gussie.

And then the embrace tightened further still; one of its winding limbs contrived to snake around her throat; and Gussie found herself deprived of air.

'Well,' she choked. 'This is embarrassing.'

THIRTEEN

After the disturbance following Theo's hunger pangs, the journey to London proceeded without further mishap. The steel chest's trio of legs, however, remained in place, and continued to twitch — and occasionally, kick — all the way to Bow Street.

'You would think they would take themselves off,' Theo remarked, when Ballantine's coach had come to a halt in the midst of a narrow street. Tall buildings loomed on either side, built edge-to-edge; since dawn had yet to break, Theo could determine little of them save a mass of shadowed, hulking presences. The effect would not have disconcerted him in the least, if he had not had rather a night of it.

'Take themselves off where?' said Ballantine, not without justice. He had shed his ogre's shape some ten minutes before, and now sat looking perfectly innocuous in contrast.

'To...' Theo groped for words. 'Wherever it was they came from.'

They sat in silence for a moment, staring down at the recalcitrant chest. It had lain on its side for the remainder of the trip, its legs (safely bound) stretched out to one side. In this forlorn posture it yet remained, neither Theo nor Ballantine having the least idea how to convey it out of the coach without being shredded for their trouble by the wicked black claws.

'No idea,' Theo finally said. 'One of the darker quarters of Hell, I should think.'

'Wait here for a moment,' said Ballantine. He had the door open in a trice, and was gone before Theo could remonstrate with him.

'What—' Theo began, but stopped when he perceived that the wretched Runner was already out of hearing. With a sigh, he slumped in his seat, weariness very much getting the better of him. He could not, when it came to it, remember the last time he had enjoyed more than a dismal three or four hours of sleep. Why, he was so tired he was hallucinating. He watched with idle interest as something long and slithering emerged from under the lid of the chest, and groped towards where he himself sat.

It brushed against his leg.

'*Ow*,' Theo gasped, for it *stung*. Then he jumped, with enough violence to set the coach rocking, and scrambled into the opposite corner of the vehicle. '*What*—' he gasped, now thoroughly awake. His trusty hatchet, thankfully, being near at hand, he grasped it in trembling fingers and hacked wildly at the protrusion.

It fell in a spray of black blood, and lay twitching.

Theo sat, rigidly alert, staring in appalled horror at the chest. Good God, they had fastened down the lid with the sturdiest of locks, and strapped it about with chains. How the Devil had the Book contrived to reach through all of that?

'Ballantine,' he croaked, then raised his voice. 'Ballantine!'

A moment passed. Theo repeated his cry.

'What is it?' came Ballantine's voice, and the coach-door was wrenched open from outside. The Runner held a lantern, the light from which flooded into the coach.

Theo wordlessly pointed at the felled... *thing* that lay on the floor.

Ballantine's mouth opened, then closed. 'Right,' he said. 'No time to waste.' He climbed back into the coach, and by the simple expedient of applying his stout boot to the side of the chest, managed to send it sailing out the door. A few solid kicks did the trick, and then he was out after it.

Theo hastened to follow.

'Grab the other side,' said Ballantine. 'But if you can manage to keep that axe handy...'

Theo tucked the axe under one arm, and applied his strength to the task of hefting the chest. It came up easily enough; the thing was not that heavy a burden for two hale young men. Moving at the briskest trot possible in their encumbered state, Theo and Ballantine hurried into the nearest of the tall, shadowed buildings, carting their reviled burden with them.

Inside, a trio of men waited. They spilled back as Ballantine came barrelling into the hall, their eyes going wide.

'Ballantine,' said one, a burly man with shaggy, greying hair and a mighty paunch. 'You said nothing about *legs*—'

'New development,' said Ballantine breathlessly. 'Shall we talk later?'

The three Runners — presumably — fell back out of the way. Ballantine led Theo towards the rear of the house, and down what seemed an interminable number of stairs.

'Cellar prison?' said Theo.

'Seems to work for you,' answered Ballantine. 'And traditions ought not to be messed with, no?'

Theo answered only with a grunt, being rather out of breath. Several more minutes passed in silence, but by the end of them, the rebellious chest had been deposited into a snug, featureless room without windows, and Theo and Ballantine had withdrawn onto the safe side of the door.

As a set of heavy iron bolts locked into place with a succession of reassuring *clangs*, Theo permitted himself a small sigh of relief.

'Your chest?' he enquired.

'I don't presently fancy trying to retrieve it,' said Ballantine. 'Do you?'

'No. I hope you were not in need of it, for I'd be surprised if you're ever to get it back.'

'Never in its original condition, to be sure.'

'Might find the legs handy. You never know.'

'I might, but I'd need a more biddable spirit to go along with them.'

Theo's smile was faint. 'No chance of that.'

'I'd say not.' He turned and began a weary ascent of the stairs. 'Drink?'

'*Please.*'

'The coach is at your disposal, when you want to return,' said Ballantine half an hour later. He sat with Theo in a tiny parlour on the second floor of the building, a cosy enough affair with wainscoting and drapes and a few perfectly good chairs. Collapsed in one of them, and with a quantity of decent scotch whisky making its way down his throat, Theo had no immediate complaints.

'I had better get back,' he said.

'Doubts about Lord Felix?' said Ballantine.

'A great many of them.'

'I am sorry to put you out of your way. But I'm glad we managed the thing.'

'Are you?' Theo drained his glass, and set it down. 'I'll be interested to know if you still feel that way tomorrow, let alone next week.'

Ballantine grimaced. 'Without the other Book at hand, surely it will be quiet enough?'

Theo gave a hollow laugh. 'Surely it won't somehow reach out of the chest we put it in and try to throttle us,' said he. 'Surely it won't *grow legs and run away.*'

Ballantine returned a look expressive of rueful disgust, downed his whisky, and coughed.

'Keep plenty of strong spirits at hand,' Theo recommended.

The heady combination of exhaustion, a sudden release of tension, and strong drink worked its usual magic upon Theo, and he fell asleep in his chair. So he assumed, anyway, for he started awake some time later to find himself alone in the parlour; Ballantine's chair was empty. A grey light filtered through the window, proclaiming that dawn had broken at last, and some time ago.

Theo took himself outside. The street — Bow Street, he presumed, though he had never had chance to confirm it — remained quiet, despite the hour being reasonably advanced; nearing noon, in fact. He had slept for a few hours, and felt somewhat the better for it, though approximately sixteen more would not go amiss.

He stood on the doorstep for some little time, watching the progress of somebody's shabby old carriage wending its way up the street, and thinking.

He must go home, of course, and soon. Lord Felix could not safely be left in charge of the Towers for long — could he? Though perhaps it was ungenerous to think it. The old lord was Theo's senior by many, *many* years, and had once been the head of the family. Perhaps his were safer hands than Theo's, especially in times of crisis.

And he was devilish hungry. His ill-fated meal in the middle of the night seemed to have taken place a decade ago, as far as his stomach was concerned. But how was he to slake his peculiar brand of thirst? No rabbits in London. Nothing of the kind.

His gaze alighted on a plump woman walking briskly past the turning into Bow Street. The winter chill had put roses into her cheeks, and her energetic step advertised a flourishing state of health.

Hardly knowing what he was doing, Theo drifted after

her.

'Hey,' said a voice, sometime later. 'Hey! Come off it, old man! Not the thing at all!'

Theo blinked, and focused.

Bow Street was gone. Turning wildly, he saw no trace of it, for he had wandered for some distance. He stood in a much larger street, lined with showy, expensive properties, and there were a great many other people milling about in the street with him.

He caught a glimpse of the plump woman with the roses in her cheeks, disappearing into the crowd.

'*Oh,*' he sighed, and cursed. 'It's just that I am so *hungry.*' And he had lost his grip on himself; dangerous, that, especially in the middle of London. If he had caught up to the woman, what would he have done? Helped himself to a drink, right there in the street? 'I shall be burned at the stake by tea time,' he sighed.

'They don't do that sort of thing nowadays,' said the voice, and Theo turned about again. 'Could find yourself in a deuced lot of trouble, though,' the voice went on, helpfully.

It belonged to a young man of Theo's own age, and he stood a prudent distance away — about four feet. He was as neat as Theo was untidy, with well-ordered golden hair, immaculate attire, and gleaming boots.

The thought filtering into Theo's thirst-fevered brain was that he recognised the fellow.

'Hargreve?' said he, blinking. 'No; I must be dreaming.'

'You're not,' said Hargreve.

'Though why I would dream up *you,* of all possible faces from the past, is beyond me to imagine.'

Hargreve seemed unfazed by this manner of greeting. 'Because you are not dreaming,' he said, dusting something invisible from the front of his dark, superbly-cut coat. 'Hello, Bedge. Lucky I ran into you. Two more minutes and you would have disgraced yourself.'

'Again?' said Theo drily. 'It doesn't often happen.'

'Then you *have* changed.'

Theo grinned, in spite of himself. 'I have, actually.'

'My felicitations, old boy. Isn't because of a lady about the house, is it?'

'No! I'm not married.'

Mr. Hargreve — William Hargreve, formerly of Northwood's School for the Wealthy and Wyrded, presently second in line to inherit the Viscountcy of Dagworth — chuckled. 'Of course not,' he agreed, affability unimpaired. 'No one would take you, I daresay.'

'Not a soul. Not if she had any wits, at any rate, and I should hardly like to wed a dribbling idiot.'

Hargreve nodded, his eyes dancing. 'That's the Bedge I remember. What *are* you doing in London?'

'When I am not preying upon unsuspecting matrons? I'm here for...' Theo paused, endeavouring, without success, to come up with a succinct explanation. 'To tell the truth, it's rather a long story.'

'And until you are fed, you haven't sufficient wit to tell it,' nodded Hargreve. 'Come along, then. Best get you a bite to eat.'

He strode off without further ado, moving with the confident step of a man who knows exactly where to go. Theo, bemused, followed.

A few minutes' walk brought them into a quite different part of London: salubrious enough, though without ostentation. Hargreve conducted Theo into a building so innocuous-looking — smooth grey stone, white-painted sash windows, a modest three storeys tall — that the place excited Theo's suspicions at once. And his instincts were not far wrong, for five minutes saw him seated before a comfortable fire in a chamber equally nondescript, with a glass of rich, red liquid set at his elbow.

Theo stared at it.

Hargreve paused his assault upon his own beverage — a duo, in fact, of coffee and beer — and raised an eyebrow in Theo's direction. 'Drink up, Bedge. It'll go cold.'

Theo seized the glass, and took a quick swallow.

It was fresh, and warm.

The rest vanished in pretty short order.

He sat for a moment afterwards, enjoying a glow of repletion.

Finally, he spoke. 'You can just... *order* it?' The words emerged in a hoarse croak; Theo's mind struggled to grasp the concept.

'Naturally,' said Hargreve, sipping coffee. 'Not from every establishment, of course, but the right places? In a trice.'

Theo blinked once, and twice. 'Do you know? I cannot think how it is that I never came to London before.'

Hargreve grinned. '*I* can. Getting you to take more than two steps beyond your own front door always was a trial. You can't have forgotten; you were a legend at Northwood. We all called you the Hermit.'

Theo grimaced, toying with the empty glass. Traces of its erstwhile contents lingered yet, staining the clear vessel a pleasing, delicate pink. 'You should try out my Wyrde sometime,' he recommended. 'Nothing has people reaching for the pitch-forks faster.'

'I never supposed that it bothered you,' said Hargreve. 'You had such a splendid air of indifference.'

'That was rather the point. Nothing could be permitted to bother me.'

Hargreve lifted his coffee in a salute. 'That's the spirit.'

Theo abandoned the conversation in favour of accosting a waiter, and ordered a second glass. Hargreve's smile, upon Theo's return to his seat, broadened.

'How long do you mean to stay?' he enquired.

'Not long.'

'No? Are you sure? If you think *that* is a wonder,' — he nodded towards Theo's empty glass — 'you'll love London.'

'There's *more?*'

Hargreve laughed. 'Stay for a week, and I'll show you.'

'A week is too long.'

'Three days, then.'

Theo nodded. 'Done.'

'Excellent.' Hargreve swallowed the rest of his coffee, and began upon his beer. 'Now, then. I believe you had a tale to tell.'

FOURTEEN

Let us return to Gussie, down in the wine-cellar at the Towers, and engaged in an inappropriately close embrace with the Book of Werth. We left her choking to death, did not we, and turning purple in the face — as Gussie herself would later confirm, *not* a predicament of any dignity.

Imagine the ire of Lord Werth, upon seeing his worst fears realised. He must not be blamed for losing his temper; indeed, anger rather fuelled his endeavours than otherwise.

'Damned disobedient *girl!*' he raged, laying into the Book like a man demented, though armed with nothing better than a bottle full of wine. This article very soon encountered its doom, being impatiently dashed to pieces upon the hard stone of the cellar floor. Wine flowed — not unlike a river of blood, Gussie thought, in a dazed kind of appreciation — and her uncle emerged with a tolerably large shard of jagged glass in his hand.

With this he slashed, and sliced, amid bellows of rage; the thing constricting Gussie's throat relaxed; and if her uncle's precision was not absolutely perfect, she would not repine over the long, shallow cut adorning her abused throat, for blessed air flowed in.

She would not, however, release her prisoner. She lay

upon the floor, the damp chill of ancient stone seeping through her clothes, her arms locked tightly around the struggling Book.

'Damn you, Gussie, let *go!*' bellowed Lord Werth.

Gussie shook her head. 'If I do, it will be gone in a trice,' she wheezed. 'And we'll have poor Oliver squeezed to bits before he can blink, or perhaps Mrs. Gosling. Or my aunt. No, I cannot let it go.' This last was uttered through gritted teeth, for the Book embarked upon a fresh struggle for freedom, and something kicked her soundly in the abdomen. 'Ouch,' she added faintly.

Lord Werth muttered something incomprehensible, but perhaps best unheard, for it could hardly be suitable language for a young lady's ears.

Then Gussie felt herself seized and borne upwards, carried in her uncle's surprisingly strong grip. He charged out of the wine-cellar with Gussie and the Book cast over one shoulder, and ran for the only room capable of containing the thing.

'Oh, my,' came Lord Felix's voice. 'Is she dead?'

'Get out of the way, Felix,' grated Lord Werth. 'She's got the Book.'

'Oh, she has! Capital. Just a moment.'

Gussie dimly perceived her disreputable ancestor blocking the passage ahead, naught but a shadowed outline; unsteady on his ruined leg, he swayed as he stood, and Gussie could not tell what he was attempting to do.

Not, that is, until a flare of light banished the darkness, bringing Lord Felix's hideous countenance into sudden view. It was stretched in a rictus grin. 'Well, look at that!' said he. 'I can still do it.'

It consisted of a small, but intensely hot flame which had come into being in the palm of Lord Felix's hand. The fire was more blue than orange, and gave off a quantity of thick smoke.

She did not have much time to admire the effect, however, for the Book had not lain idle in her arms.

'Uncle?' she choked, and coughed.

The thing freshly wound around her neck *squeezed*.

'*Felix!*' raged Lord Werth. 'Get out of the way!'

He did not wait for Lord Felix to obey this command, but barrelled forward; if the corpse would not move himself out of the way, Lord Werth would simply go through him.

But several things happened at once.

The grip on Gussie's neck tightened inexorably, until she saw stars.

Lord Felix leapt forward with a cry of triumph, the flame in his hands roaring high.

And something… *screamed*.

It was the Book, which fought like a wild thing in Gussie's arms; and this time she was obliged to let go of it, in spite of all her heroic inclinations, for the Book was luxuriously, exhilaratingly on fire.

'Go, go!' carolled Lord Felix, dancing about in demented triumph. 'We'll be safe now! Look at the thing *burn!*'

It was, indeed, burning; very thoroughly at that. It lay in a screaming heap upon the floor, engulfed in its own personal inferno, and as Gussie watched, its covers blackened at the edges.

Her only regret was for the records it contained, which must now be forever lost. Everything else in her heart might more accurately be termed a vindictive satisfaction.

'Felix,' said Lord Werth. 'You'd better put it out.' He had not shouted, but in his voice was an intensity that carried almost as well.

'Well, I shan't,' said Lord Felix, still beaming. 'It's the best fire I've had this age.'

'It is a very good fire,' said Lord Werth. 'Too good, Felix. Put it out.'

As the old lord stubbornly shook his head, Gussie perceived, as in a dream, that the hem of her dress had developed its very own wreath of flame.

Sense returned to her dazed wits in a rush. With a shriek, she kicked. Her uncle, reaching the same realisation, batted furiously at the fire, but only succeeded in spreading the flames to his own garments.

Indeed, the fire was spreading *everywhere*. What it found to feed upon, Gussie could not imagine, for naught existed down here but dust and cobwebs and stone. Nonetheless, a curtain of flame roared down the passage, reaching greedily for anything in its path.

And Lord Felix went up like a torch.

Swearing horribly, Lord Werth abandoned the Book and Lord Felix both, and took off at a run. He dashed straight *though* the wall of fire, screaming something Gussie could not make out; she had time only to tightly shut her eyes, a miserably ineffective defence, and in a horrific surge of killing heat they were *through* and into the relative cool of the cellar stairs.

Lord Werth charged up them, breathing hard. At the top, he and Gussie fell in a tangle of limbs and she found herself seized, and rolled furiously over and over upon the floor.

She heard her aunt's voice, dimly, expressing some natural alarm; and through it all, the sound of Lord Felix somewhere below, laughing.

'Come, get up,' said Lord Werth, and she was hauled upright, and pushed into her aunt's arms. 'We must get outside. The fire won't stop.'

Until the Towers are turned to ash. Gussie heard the rest of her uncle's sentence unfurl within her own mind. With an effort, she withdrew from her aunt's supporting embrace, and found that she could stand. 'The servants,' she croaked, coughing upon smoke, her abused throat burning. 'I'll go for Mrs. Gosling.' Thank goodness she had dismissed Frosty to the cottage.

Lord Werth, soot-stained and burned and grim, nodded. 'Five minutes,' he said. 'Anyone you have not found in that time, leave them.'

Gussie swallowed, nodded her acknowledgement, and took off at a run.

All things considered, Lady Werth ought to have known better than to grieve for Lord Felix.

Not that she was doing any particularly admirable job of it.

'*Fool* of a corpse!' lamented she. 'If he must go and burn himself alive, he need not have taken half the Towers with him!'

'Nothing could burn Lord Felix *alive*, Aunt,' Gussie pointed out, without much effect.

The sorry rabble presently representing the noble House of Werth had gathered on the front lawn, from which vantage point they had an excellent view of the damage Lord Felix (and the Book of Werth) had wrought. By the time morning came at last, the fires were largely quenched, the airborne efforts of Great-Aunt Honoria and Great-Uncle Silvester having had something to do with this. Rather more of the ancient house was standing than anybody had expected, in the hopeless hours just before dawn. Still, the façade gaped unattractively, having lost such accessories as doors, windows and most of the roof. Inside, the unflinching eye might discern a distinct lack of furniture and other such trappings, not to mention a horrifying quantity of soot.

The aerial survey of the aforementioned duo confirmed that the worst was not so *very* bad as all that: 'More than half the house is gone!' Great-Aunt Honoria announced upon her return, in the process revealing that slightly less than half the house yet remained.

'I could fancy a game of billiards,' said Great-Uncle Silvester, perching amongst the gravel of the wide (and undamaged) driveway.

Gussie wondered briefly whether this was intended to mean that the billiard-room had survived, and dismissed the question as immaterial.

Aunt Werth, ordinarily stout-hearted enough, and not lacking in resources, found herself unequal to the demands of that morning. She had entirely lost her composure, and though she had not carried this quite to the point of making an icicle of herself, the frost glittered copiously in her dishevelled hair, and her face was unnaturally white. She sat slumped in a graceless posture among the damp and muddy grass, heedless of the damage to her gown.

Lord Werth stood nearby, having long since abandoned his attempts to raise his wife up from her unhelpful posture upon the floor. He was unnaturally still, and troubled; deep lines seemed graven about his mouth overnight, and he had not stopped frowning. His clothes were in a disreputable state, partially torn and partially burned, and he had suffered some fire damage to his leg, for the flesh there was blistered and red-raw.

Gussie was engaged in pacing a muddy furrow into the grass. She was on the move, partly because of an insurmountable degree of restlessness; the sudden and near total loss of one's ancestral abode *will* have an effect upon the nerves, however steady they might ordinarily be, and this must be especially true if the event was preceded by a fight to the near-death with the Book.

The other reason was simply that she was in pain. The wretched Book had done her a deal of harm, and she felt a mass of bruises from head to toe. The application of a small inferno thereafter had added some raw, stinging pains to the mix, on account of which her feelings about Lord Felix were not much more forgiving than her aunt's. Sitting motionless in the cold only exaggerated this general effect, and so she walked.

'If he *were* alive he would not be so for long,' said Aunt Werth, expanding upon her general anti-Felix theme. 'I would trample him where he stood. Drop great boulders upon his *head*. Throw him into the deepest, darkest pit and—'

She stopped at this promising point because her

attention — indeed, everyone's attention — was turned elsewhere.

A figure had emerged from the ruins of the Towers. He came towards them at an ambling, shambling gait, and as he neared the miserable trio the abominable creature actually *smiled.*

'Good morning,' said Lord Felix, making his bow. He straightened, and made as if to draw in a great breath of air, though he had no longer the lungs with which to do it. '*Excellent* weather,' said he, casting a satisfied glance at the clear, cold sky.

Gussie was intrigued to observe that the fire had done away with what was left of his flesh. He was a burned wreck of a skeleton, quite free of garments, but in no way in need of them, for every defining feature was gone.

Even this could not faze him.

'If there is one thing I regret in all of this,' Gussie said into the speechless silence, 'it's that I never thought *before* to ask what your Wyrde was.' His status as a walking corpse had misled her, she supposed; in that state, he was supernatural enough. It had not entered her head to consider that this state of being was her uncle's work, not a natural quality of Felix's own.

'Oh?' said Felix. 'I ought to have done it sooner, of course. You're quite right.'

'Burned down the Towers *sooner*?' choked Lady Werth.

'The Book,' Felix explained, and cast a careless glance behind himself at the ruined wreck. 'Used to have better control,' he confided. 'But I'm a bit out of practice.'

'Aunt…' Gussie said, in what she hoped was a soothing way, for poor Lady Werth visibly hovered on the edge of a complete and total icing. And that would be *just* what they'd need — Aunt Werth an insensate block of ice for days together. Though perhaps she would prefer to miss the immediate aftermath of the fire.

She retained control of herself, however, rather to Gussie's admiration, for much lesser things had been known to overset her in the past. 'Felix,' she said, in a tightly controlled voice. 'I think it's time you went back to bed.'

Gussie expected a vehement demurral from Lord Felix, but to her surprise he gave a weak laugh, and collapsed in a heap upon the floor. He sat there for some time, wheezing and giggling and shaking his head. 'Quite right,' he said at last. 'I could use a nap.' With which words he hauled himself upright again, and shambled off in the general direction of the churchyard.

Lord Werth followed him in silence.

'I am just glad,' said Lady Werth after a while, 'that no one was seriously hurt.'

Gussie was also thankful for it. Mrs. Gosling and Oliver and the rest of the servants had all been got out safely, and had subsequently dispersed into the village in search of alternative accommodations. The Werths only had remained with the house, perhaps in hopes that Honoria and Silvester might be able to save most of it.

Miss Frostell had slept through the event.

'And that the Book is *gone*,'added Lady Werth.

Gussie had no trouble agreeing with this sentiment either.

Lord Werth returned soon afterwards, muddied and weary.

'Is he finished?' said Lady Werth.

'Yes.'

'For good?'

'Cannot promise.'

A short sigh answered him, and then her ladyship levered herself to her feet. 'Well,' she said crisply. 'It probably *was* about time we new-furnished the drawing-rooms.'

Lord Werth mustered the faintest of smiles. 'I am sure they will look charming.'

'In the meantime, we shall adjourn to Gussie's cottage.'

'I shall be delighted to offer refreshments and a rest,

Aunt,' said Gussie. 'But I do not imagine you will want to stay there for very long. I have only a single spare room, and it is quite — well, it is cramped.'

'I am not so fine a lady as all that,' said Lady Werth, rather shortly.

Gussie, with rare tact, refrained from pointing out how little *she* enjoyed the idea of her tiny cottage all cluttered up with extra people. She would not mind it at all, for a few days; but for months together? No.

'The town house?' said Lord Werth. Weariness or pain or anger — or all three — had robbed him of full sentences for the present.

Lady Werth paused. 'I had forgotten. Is it in a habitable condition?'

Lord Werth merely looked at the Towers. His mouth twitched, perhaps with a dark sort of humour.

'I see your point,' said his wife.

'If one might enquire,' said Gussie politely, 'which town it is in?'

'London,' said Lady Werth, looking at Gussie as though she were an intriguing species of idiot.

'Ah, of course,' murmured Gussie. '*The* town.' Her wayward heart fluttered a little with an excitement she did not choose to display, and she made no effort to quell the feeling. London! Where Theo had gone, and Ballantine. Where Gussie had never expected to go in her life.

She emerged from a brief but fervent daydream of her imminent London life to find both her aunt and uncle looking at her. Narrowly. Suspiciously.

'Come now,' she said, with her most winning smile. 'You cannot imagine I shall be so disobliging as to misbehave?'

Neither of them spoke. Lord Werth's brows were perhaps seen to ascend a fraction towards his hairline.

Gussie sighed. 'I shall have Frosty with me,' she pointed out. 'A paragon of propriety—'

'An incorrigible enabler,' said Lady Werth.

'—under whose guidance I have no doubt I shall comport myself admirably.'

Lady Werth's expression turned steely.

'If it will make you feel better, I shall remain all the time with you,' Gussie offered. 'Except when I am sleeping, of course. I am to have my own bedchamber?'

Lady Werth took a deep, fortifying breath. 'I remember when life was simple,' she said, presumably to her husband.

But Lord Werth's mouth twitched again. He glanced at the bright winter sky, then at the burned-out Towers, and said: 'Do you happen to remember when that was?'

FIFTEEN

The town house in question was not, at that moment, quite as empty as Lord and Lady Werth imagined.

Their son Lord Bedgberry, newly a man-about-town, had found himself desirous of remaining in London, yet without any obvious place of abode. Happily or unhappily, his memory had dredged up a dim recollection of the place, just as Lord Werth's had done.

The house had been in the Werth family for generations, of course, but the family had not been much in the habit of using it for the last two or three of those. London was not always kind to the Wyrded; that's what had sometimes been said, when the subject of the capital had come up.

Theo was finding it rather otherwise.

On the afternoon following his interception by Hargreve, Theo had ventured to pay a visit to the Werths' erstwhile party-spot, and had found it firmly shut up, with the knocker off the door. Probably it had languished in so ignominious a state for over a decade.

The address was not especially fashionable, as anyone less ignorant than Theo could have told him; not that this information would have weighed with him at all.

What did weigh with him was the lack of a key, for he

hadn't had the forethought to retrieve it from his father.

'Well,' said Hargreve, standing with Theo on the freezing street outside the impregnable house. 'Hotel then?'

But Theo was not to be so easily discouraged. He made his way around to the rear of the house, and set up such a clamour upon the back door as must surely be heard several doors down. If anyone remained inside, they could not fail to be disturbed by it.

It nonetheless took some few minutes before he heard the rattling of an ancient doorknob turning, and the stout door swung slowly open.

On the other side stood an elderly woman as dusty and moth-eaten as the rest of the house, though the arrangement of her hair and garments declared her essential respectability. She squinted suspiciously at Theo. 'And who might you be?'

Theo took no offence at this ungracious attitude. He had arrived unannounced and unintroduced, and had been so eccentric as to present himself at the door customarily reserved for servants. Nothing about *his* appearance could present him as such, however, despite his generally unkempt state.

'Wants a lick of paint, I should think,' he said, nodding at the door.

'*You* try telling his lordship that,' said the woman, and made to close the door on him.

'No, wait,' said Theo, quickly getting his foot in the way of the door before it could slam on him. 'I am his lordship.'

She froze, staring at him. 'What? Lord Werth *dead*? I've heard nothing of it.'

This news appeared to affect her more than Theo might have expected, for she clutched at the doorframe with trembling hands, and her papery-white complexion turned whiter still.

'Good God, no!' Theo said hastily. 'I mean, I'm Lord

Bedgberry. His son?'

The afflicted woman — housekeeper? — took a breath. 'I see.'

'I am staying here,' he enlarged.

'Ah?'

'I suppose there is food, and whatnot?'

The housekeeper looked narrowly at him. 'If what I remember of your lordship's right, you won't be wanting any ordinary kind of food.'

Theo smiled, showing his teeth.

This vision might ordinarily be counted upon to horrify, but the housekeeper merely nodded, and stepped back, opening the door wider. 'Come in, then. Though what sort of a lark you was kicking up, showing yourself at the servants' entrance, I'm sure I don't know.'

'Had no key,' Theo said briefly as he stepped inside. The room beyond proved to be rather bare and freezingly cold; he shivered. 'And someone's taken the door-knocker off the front.'

'Bit of a provincial, are we, my lord? *That* indicates that the family is not presently in residence.'

Theo nodded. 'Any chance we could put it back on?'

The house was in a deplorable state, Theo later reflected, having been set up in as decent a bedchamber as the obliging Mrs. Gavell could arrange for him. Everything smelled of mildew and dust, the carpets were tatty, and nothing new had likely been brought into the house for at least fifty years.

'Hotel, then?' said Hargreve again, upon surveying these unpromising signs.

'What? Not a chance,' said Theo, perfectly at home. 'What more could I need?'

Hargreve looked long at his former schoolfriend, and Mrs. Gavell's words floated back through Theo's brain. *Provincial, are we?*

'Well?' he said. 'What is it?'

164

'We are going,' said Hargreve, 'to Stebbington's.'

Thus began a heady few days of idle dissipation such as Theo had never known, for Stebbington's proved to be a gentlemen's club catering exclusively to the Wyrded gentry.

What *delight*.

Somewhere in the midst of his second visit there, surrounded by those whose interest in his Wyrde was merely friendly, and not appalled, Theo remembered what Gussie had said to him not so long ago.

Somehow or other, he had at last developed *cronies*.

He felt an odd impulse to write to her and tell her all about it, but dismissed the idea as absurd. She would only hassle him to *use* said cronies for some mischievous purpose of her own, doubtless to do with the damned Book; and he had had more than enough of that creature for the time being.

Still, he looked forward to sharing this development when he returned to the Towers. It was just possible that she might even be a little bit... pleased with him.

The three days passed quickly, as Theo paid several visits to Stebbington's, and also to a range of dining-spots catering to precisely his tastes; not to mention a theatre at which the finest of Wyrded performers put the best of their abilities upon display. Late one afternoon, as Theo lingered at the town-house only long enough to complete his toilet (for he proposed to go back to this eye-opening theatre that very evening with Hargreve, and a handsome red-headed actress had happened to catch his eye), there came a brisk and business-like knock upon the front door.

Theo frowned. That was not Hargreve's knock.

Two or three minutes later, a light tap sounded upon his own dressing-room door, and a weary-looking maid appeared.

'Gentleman to see you, my lord,' she said with a bob of a curtsey.

'Hargreve, is it?' said Theo, for who else could it possibly be?

'Gave his name as Ballantine, sir,' said the maid, and went away.

Ballantine! Theo had all but forgotten him. With a snarl of frustration (for he foresaw that a visit from the Runner would probably destroy all his hopeful plans for the evening), he dashed downstairs, and found Mr. Ballantine awaiting him in the hastily spruced-up parlour.

'I see that I am disturbing you,' said Ballantine, taking in Theo's unusually immaculate evening-dress.

'Somewhat,' Theo agreed, lightly touching the fine cloth of his coat. The costume had but just arrived from a tailor Hargreve had recommended, and he had not had it on for more than half an hour. To his own surprise, he liked it. He liked it a lot.

'Going somewhere?' pursued Ballantine.

'Strangewayes,' said Theo.

Ballantine asked no questions, merely nodding; of course, he would be familiar with the theatre. 'I have some news that may interest you,' he said. 'If you can spare me a few minutes?'

'It couldn't have gone in a letter?' said Theo.

Ballantine's brows rose. Then, stiffly, he bowed. 'Apologies for disturbing your lordship,' he said, with a stilted and deliberate courtesy, and made to leave.

'Hold, man, hold,' said Theo. 'I didn't mean to dismiss you. I *meant*, it must be something… urgent?'

'Something interesting, at any rate,' said Ballantine, mollified. 'As to how urgent it is, we'll see.'

'Sit down,' said Theo, nodding to the nearest arm-chair. 'And let's hear it.'

'I might have mentioned I had a man working on the matter of Cruikshank and Wirt?' said Ballantine, not taking the seat.

'You did. Ah! Yes! You've got something?'

Ballantine's answering look was measuring in some

way. 'I have,' he said slowly.

'You begin to terrify me,' said Theo. 'The news is bad, I collect?'

'The name "Wirt",' said Ballantine. 'Has nothing occurred to you?'

'Why should it?' said Theo. 'I said in my letter, I believe, that I had not the resources to—'

'And you haven't looked into it, since you came to London?'

'Ah…' Theo coughed. 'I haven't given the matter any thought.'

'I can see that.' Ballantine appeared more amused than judgemental; Theo's hackles rose, and then settled. 'Well, my man's got something that may interest you.'

'Please, Ballantine, just let me have it. I cannot bear the suspense.'

'Wirt,' said Ballantine. 'Add one more letter to the end, my lord, and what have you got?'

Theo thought. 'Wirte,' he tried. 'Wirtle… no, that's two. Wirt…h… Wirth?' His breath stopped, and started again in a choked gasp. 'You cannot mean—'

'I'm afraid I do. Do you see now why I was hesitant to tell you before?' Ballantine watched Theo with the careful attention of a creature uncertain as to whether or not it was about to be messily preyed upon; Theo realised he was baring his teeth in the kind of grimace he typically reserved for emergencies.

He controlled himself with an effort.

'An intriguing notion,' he finally said, passably composed. 'How came you by it?'

'The idea occurred to me some time ago,' said Ballantine. '*Werth* is not so common a name, after all. I had Henshawe go through everything there is to find about your family, and the Towers. Do you want to hear it?'

Theo *really* did not, but he made himself nod anyway.

'Long ago,' said Ballantine, 'by which I mean some few centuries in the past, public feeling about those afflicted

167

with the Wyrde was not so accommodating as it is now.'

'Accommodating?' Theo spluttered. 'Surely you must know—'

'Relatively speaking, my lord,' said Ballantine mildly. 'It is some time since anyone has been sent to the stake for it, after all.'

Theo's mouth tightened. He nodded. 'Sorry. Go on.'

'Some few individuals were particularly, ah, vigorous in their pursuit of — of those termed *witches*. One of them was a man called Ademar Wirt. He was extraordinarily successful; such records as there are suggest he was responsible for the burning of over a hundred men and women.'

Theo blanched. 'All Wyrded?'

'Probably not, no. Among them were doubtless many who were simply unlucky. That point, however, is immaterial for our purposes. What interests *us* is the case of Avice Haye, known as Mother Ave.'

At this point, Ballantine stopped speaking, and took a scrap of paper out of a pocket in his red waist-coat. This he handed to Theo.

Theo gazed at it in some confusion. 'What's this? A song?'

'Aye, sir. A song, in which Mother Ave is remembered.'

Old Mother Ave did her neyghbours hir name,
The Beldame of Gleucestre, a wytch was she;
Dead corpsis from eyrth could she uprote,
An inchantresse beyond compare.

Theo looked up from the note, not much enlightened. 'She had Father's Wyrde,' he observed.

'So it appears, and perhaps more besides.'

'I, er, do not see what this has to do with Ademar Wirt.'

'He burned her,' said Ballantine.

'Oh.'

'And it seems she really was an *inchantresse beyond compare,* for she's said to have cursed him for it as she died.'

Theo grimaced. 'Death-curses are... not good,' he said cautiously.

'Well, that's as it happens. This particular death-curse decreed that Ademar Wirt, and *all his descendaunts, shall be as Wyrde as I am.*'

'What.'

'Or specifically, that they shall *suffyr the Wyrde in its gretest degree, until Time shall have run oute, and the Earth shalle darkene and fayl.*'

Theo blinked. 'That's... a long time.'

'And furthermore, *that the Wyrde shall descynd 'pon evry Wirt when the babe reachyth its thyrde year, and nevyrmore shall it departe.*'

Theo, finding that his knees had suddenly turned watery, groped for a chair, and sank into it.

Ballantine paused, but Theo found nothing to say into the heavy silence.

'So you see, my lord,' said the Runner at last, 'I think we have solved a little mystery here. Or did you never wonder how it comes about that every Werth becomes Wyrded at exactly their third birthday?'

'Not very much,' Theo admitted, collecting himself. 'It is simply what is.' He frowned, and lifted a finger. 'But — forgive me, but as interesting as this is, we were speaking of Cruikshank and Wirt, and the Books—'

'There is more,' admitted Ballantine. 'Would your lordship like a spot of brandy first?'

'What? No.' Theo shook himself. 'I am well enough, though I collect I look ghastly.'

'Utterly,' said Ballantine. 'Though that's no so very uncommon, I suppose.'

'I *am* a Werth,' Theo agreed. 'Or, apparently, a *Wirt.*'

'Aye, well. Ademar Wirt, and his father before him, had partnered with the Gloucestershire Cruikshank we have already discovered, and created these Books. And here they are guilty of a touch of hypocrisy, for they must have had the assistance of somebody powerfully Wyrded in order to do it. Who could have consented to lend themselves to the creation of Books designed to *destroy* the Wyrded, I cannot tell you; perhaps they were compelled. However it was, the Books came into being with the sole purpose of extending the Wirts' reach.'

'This was before the burning of Mother Ave, and the death-curse?'

'Some years before. Well, time passes, as time is wont to do. The Books are slowly spread about England, and beyond, though perhaps never very many of them. They cannot have been easy to create. And as time passes, *Wirt* becomes *Werth,* and through service to Queen Elizabeth they enter the nobility.'

'Must be around then that the Towers were built,' Theo put in.

'The oldest parts, certainly. So we have a noble and unusually Wyrded family, with a half-forgotten history of persecuting what's now become their own kind. And a Book, a family heirloom, passed down from your ancestors…'

'You would think,' said Theo, 'that something as horrific as the Book of Werth would have been expunged long since.'

'Save for their habit of sometimes behaving themselves,' said Ballantine drily. 'Almost anything can be forgotten in time, my lord.'

'And we are talking of hundreds of years,' sighed Theo. 'Good God, what a tale.'

'What do you now think to do with the Book?' said Ballantine. 'Now that you know?'

'Isn't up to me. Have you told this to my mother and father?'

'Not yet. I thought to ask what you'd prefer me to do.'

Theo raised a brow.

'Shall I write to them, or would you rather such news

170

came from you?'

Theo pictured his mother's probable reaction to the story, and sighed. 'I had better tell them.'

He thought he detected a fleeting expression on Ballantine's face that might be termed relief. 'As you wish,' said the Runner neutrally.

'I *had* better be getting home,' admitted Theo. 'Tomorrow.'

'After Strangewayes?' said Ballantine, with a glimmer of amusement.

'After Strangewayes. Hargreve will be wondering what's become of me.'

'I'll be off back to Bow Street, then,' said Ballantine.

'You are well out of this mess.' Theo rather envied the Runner that much.

'I'm not out of it,' Ballantine said. 'It is my job to deal with the curse-book.' He paused on his way out of the door, and added, 'Besides, according to your Lord Felix's ritual, I, too, am descended from Ademar Wirt.'

Two days later, having torn himself away from the surprising delights of the capital with a palpable reluctance, Theo arrived home. His hired chaise drew to a slow stop halfway up the driveway, to his puzzlement, and though he waited a couple of minutes, nobody opened the door.

He did this himself, emerging with his back to the Towers. 'Hallo?' he called up to the driver. 'What's afoot?'

The driver said nothing, was not even looking at Theo; his attention was all focused upon the Towers.

Theo, turning about, received an eyeful of the burned ruin that had once been his home.

Fully two minutes passed before he spoke.

'What *happened?*' he croaked.

Not that he needed to ask; he wasted very little thought upon the matter before he hit upon the most likely answer.

The Book of Werth had happened.

It is my job to deal with the curse-book. Ballantine's voice returned to Theo's thoughts, attended by a new thrill of horror.

'Good God,' he said faintly. 'Shall he deal with the curse-book, or shall it deal with *him*?'

'Perhaps you won't be staying, sir?' called the driver.

'No—on no account drive off—I shall be returning to London directly.'

The driver touched his hat.

What the blazes had happened to the family — there was a question to occupy all of Theo's thoughts. Had anyone been hurt?

Had anyone *survived?*

The latter question brought him out in a cold sweat just thinking about it. Where were his mother and father? Where was Gussie? If they were well, surely they would have written to tell him—

Well, but, they did not know where to write *to*, did they? He hadn't bothered to send them his direction.

He shook himself, dismissing these dark thoughts as best he could, and made a difficult decision in an instant. If his family had died in the fire, there was nothing he could do for them now. If they had not, well, they were more than capable of managing for themselves.

What he could, and must, do, was warn Ballantine.

He strode back to the carriage, and wrenched open the door. 'Back to London,' he called up to the driver. 'Quick as you can.'

SIXTEEN

In the end, the Werth family's arrival in London was not the exciting event Gussie had sometimes dreamed of. The party that drew up outside the house in Hanover Place made for a dispirited bunch. Lady Werth had not spoken a word all day, Lord Werth barely a syllable or two; even Gussie and Miss Frostell had been little disposed for conversation. Numbed with weariness and shock, and in some cases the injuries incurred during (and immediately before) the fire, no one had the energy to attempt a brightening of the mood.

No one except for Great-Aunt Honoria, that is — in a manner of speaking.

'We are far better off without the Book,' she said, and kept saying it, approximately thrice an hour, until Gussie could cheerfully have eviscerated her. Not even the observation that they were obliged to manage without the Towers, too, could dim her satisfaction.

And, 'I wish I had burned it when I was alive,' said she, at similarly regular intervals. 'How much trouble might have been saved!'

And, '*What* a good blaze it was! Felix did a superb job, now, did not he?'

To the latter observation, nobody troubled to reply at all.

By the time the coach drew up at the town-house, Gussie was desperate to get away from this rain of desultory observations. The one thing Lady Werth had mentioned was the sorry state the house was likely to be in, and the inconvenience of being obliged to appear at the house with scarcely any notice sent to Mrs. Gavell. But by

173

the time the coach had rolled to a stop, a small stream of people were erupting from the house: a footman to open the door and help the ladies down; another footman to unload their luggage (what there was of it), and carry it into the house; and then an elderly lady, which Gussie took to be Mrs. Gavell herself, actually coming out of the house to welcome them, despite the biting chill of a late morning in January.

'What a fortunate chance that his lordship should have happened to visit,' she chattered, curtseying. 'You'll find the house in much better state than could have been hoped for, a week gone.'

'His lordship?' said Lady Werth blankly. Gussie, misliking the unhealthy pallor of her aunt's skin, hovered at her elbow, poised to arrest any sudden descent towards the pavement.

'Lord Bedgberry, my lady,' said Mrs. Gavell. 'What a fine young man he's grown into, to be sure! He—'

'Theo?' interjected Lady Werth. 'Theo is here?'

'He's not here now, ma'am. Went away home, he did, and not long since either.'

Lady Werth briefly closed her eyes. 'We must have passed him somewhere on the road,' she sighed.

Gussie winced, picturing the homecoming poor Theo was in for. 'No help for it now, Aunt,' she said. 'We can send word of our whereabouts, as soon as we are settled.'

Lady Werth merely nodded, and permitted herself to be escorted into the house.

There followed the obligatory half-hour of chaos, by the end of which refreshments had been delivered, bedchambers assigned, faces washed, road-soiled garments changed, and pallid aunts thrust bodily into arm-chairs.

Not for long were they destined to enjoy a subsequent state of relative peace, however, for there came a series of assaults upon the door-knocker.

The first proved to be a gleaming young man with golden hair, and an attention to dress Gussie had never observed in anyone before. He was immaculate from head to toe, and he was standing in *their* hallway, eyeing Gussie with interest as she came rattling down the stairs. The footman who had answered the door discretely withdrew.

'Oh!' said she, stopping halfway down. And then, '*Oh*, you must be expecting to find Theo? I am sorry, but he is not here.'

The young man mulled this over, still smiling. 'Now that you mention it, he did say something about going home. I did not think he would go through with it.'

'Go through with it?' Gussie repeated, frowning. 'You make it sound as though it were a hard duty.'

'But it was,' the man assured her.

'That cannot possibly be true. Theo is only comfortable at home.' Belatedly, she made a curtsey, and added, 'We haven't been introduced, but I am Miss Werth.'

'Bedge's cousin, I collect,' came the answer, followed by a graceful bow. 'William Hargreve. Lord Bedgberry and I were at school together.'

'Bedge,' echoed Gussie wonderingly. 'Goodness, you almost persuade me that Theo once contrived to make friends.'

That won her a smile, and a surprised laugh. 'He was not so very bad,' he said.

Gussie's only response was a look of pronounced scepticism.

'Very well, perhaps he was,' Mr. Hargreve allowed. 'But then, so was I.'

'I am not sure I believe it of you. You look far too well-behaved.'

'Looks may be deceiving. *You* do not present any very alarming appearance, yet I have it on excellent authority that you are a menace to society.'

'Theo said that?' Gussie nodded. 'He is perfectly right.'

The smile returned. 'Well, if I am not to find Lord Bedgberry then I shall take myself off,' he decided. 'For I can hardly take *you* to the theatre.'

'On the contrary, I should like it of all things. I am here with my aunt and uncle, you know, and my companion. We shall make a perfectly respectable party.'

'Then may I expect to see you at Strangewayes, tomorrow night? At eight?'

'Better make it Friday,' Gussie said. 'We are all in a flutter, and it's just possible my aunt will not quite be in the mood for entertainment for a day or two.'

'I hope nothing too untoward has happened?'

'Our house has burnt down,' replied Gussie, coolly rearranging her shawl.

Mr. Hargreve looked closely at her. 'A disaster which does not appear to have much discomposed you, Miss Werth?'

'You are quite mistaken,' said Gussie politely. 'We only narrowly escaped being baked alive, and prior to that I was almost choked to death. It has been *such* an exciting week.'

Mr. William Hargreve stared. 'Bedge really was not joking me about you, was he?'

This visitor did not prove so unwelcome an interruption, then, but he had not been gone more than an hour or so before the next pounding-upon-the-door came to shatter the quiet.

The hurried (or harried) gentleman upon the other side proved to be Mr. Ballantine. He came in demanding Theo — 'Though I scarcely hope to find him, for he *did* say he would be—ah!' Mr. Ballantine's gaze alighted upon Gussie, who had gone from the parlour into the hall the moment she had heard his voice. 'Miss Werth, I had not expected — is your cousin still here?'

'No, he is not. We are told he has gone home.'

'You haven't seen him?'

'I'm afraid not. Was it especially important that I should?'

It occurred to her that Mr. Ballantine was looking scarcely better than her aunt. He had a sick look about

176

him, as though several very heavy something-or-others weighed upon his soul all at once. 'What is the matter?' she said, when he did not immediately reply.

Mr. Ballantine sagged where he stood. 'Then you have heard nothing about Ademar Wirt, and on top of all of that the damned — forgive me, the *abominable* — curse-book is gone.'

'Gone?' said Gussie sharply. 'Gone from where?'

'The extremely secure room at Bow Street where I had left it. Most unwisely, as it turns out. Bolts aplenty we had, but the hinges proved more susceptible to pressure than I had expected.' He paused. 'They appear to have been, ah, melted.'

For a moment, it was as much as Gussie could do to draw in air.

'Unwelcome news, I know,' said Mr. Ballantine grimly.

'No,' said Gussie. 'I mean, yes, it is, but I fear you don't understand just how bad this news is.'

Mr. Ballantine's gaze sharpened. 'What? What's happened?'

Gussie told him.

'The *Towers?*' he repeated, staring at her in horror. '*Burned down?*'

'Not all of it, but a fair proportion.'

'The Book of Werth burned down the *Towers?*'

'No, not quite. It was Lord Felix who started the fire, but it was because of the Book. And to be perfectly honest, the unfortunate outcome notwithstanding, I do not know that he was wrong to do so. *Nothing* could pacify the Book, in that state, and I might myself have been—' She broke off, unwilling to finish her sentence.

'You might have been killed,' said Mr. Ballantine.

'I am sure I would have thought of something,' she said, stoutly.

'I am not.' He waved away Gussie's attempts to defend her personal valour in combat, and went on: 'What concerns me is what that curse-book is likely to do now, when it's loose somewhere on the streets of London.'

'You were hoping Theo could help you to find it?'

'No. I've got every Runner I could get my hands on searching for it, and the Watch besides. No, I wanted Lord Bedgberry to help me to subdue the thing.'

'I am not sure he could,' said Gussie. 'Splitting those Books up seems to have sent them mad.'

Mr. Ballantine's face fell. 'I must tender my sincere apologies for that, Miss Werth.'

'What? Why?'

'Because *I* am the one who split up the Books.'

'That does not mean that the fire is your fault. Is that what is in your head?'

He pressed his lips together, and gave a tight nod.

'Not your fault,' Gussie said crisply. 'If you had not done it, someone else would have, soon enough.'

'It isn't important now,' he said, probably more to himself than to Gussie. 'Miss Werth, I beg of you. Do you have some idea of how to get the thing under control?'

'Without performing a re-enactment of the Great Fire?'

'If most of London is still standing by the end of this week, I shall be well pleased.'

'I hardly know,' said Gussie. 'Only Lord Felix's fire seems to have had the desired effect on *our* Book, and it is the sort of fire that is difficult to contain.'

'As opposed to mere ordinary, biddable fire,' said Mr. Ballantine, nodding.

Gussie, her pleasant dreams of attending the theatre with Mr. Hargreve wafting away, sighed. 'I will ask my uncle and aunt. Both of my aunts, in fact, and Frosty too — why not? Perhaps between us, we can come up with something.'

'I can ask no more. If several of the most Wyrded heads in the country cannot prove a match for a single Book, then we are doomed anyway.' On which cheerful thought, he bowed — but he turned away only to turn back again, and rapidly he said: 'I had perhaps better tell you what your cousin was going to convey. Who knows but that it might prove helpful.'

'Oh?' said Gussie politely.

'It is about the Books, and about your family.'

'*Our* family.'

'Our family.'

The tale of Ademir Wirt and Old Mother Ave was quickly told, and left Gussie feeling as winded as though she had been bodily socked in the gut (a feeling with which she was now passingly familiar, thanks to the Book).

'How… how *wicked* of us!' said she, and once the initial shock had passed, she began, inevitably, to laugh.

'You appear to relish the thought more than I had expected, Miss Werth,' said Mr. Ballantine.

Gussie, beaming, contrived to regain control of her face. 'It is a splendid tale, though, is it not?'

Mr. Ballantine's stare turned rather fixed.

'You had not imagined that I might be distressed, had you?' said Gussie. 'Really, if you have not grown accustomed to my ways by now, I begin to fear it will never happen.'

A slight cough answered her. 'Your… aunt, and uncle?'

'Will find it very interesting,' said Gussie politely.

In spite of himself, Mr. Ballantine chuckled.

'You need not worry that my aunt will go off in a swoon, or— oh!' She stood a moment, arrested, as another idea filtered into her thoughts. 'Then it *was* our doing,' she said,

'If you expect me to follow,' said Mr. Ballantine stiffly, 'I'm afraid I will be needing more detail.'

'You are displeased with me,' said Gussie, making a discovery. It was the rigidity of his countenance that gave it away.

'Disconcerted only,' said Mr. Ballantine. 'It is not the same thing.'

Gussie acknowledged this point with an inclination of her head. 'We have just come from Starminster,' said she, 'where the corpse of Lady Muriel Selwyn told us that *we* had once bestowed just such a Book upon her family as we possess ourselves. I could not begin to imagine how that came about, but now…'

'That fact makes some little sense,' agreed Mr. Ballantine. 'Though it was not really the Werths; more what you were before. If this news can be of use to you, Miss Werth, then I am profoundly thankful I had the opportunity to relay it.' He bowed again, and took himself off, promising to send word should any trace of the curse-book be found.

Gussie, the germ of an idea unfurling in her mind, went off in search of Lord Werth.

'I hope you are feeling well-rested, Uncle,' said Gussie, half an hour later, having relayed Mr. Ballantine's findings with suitable relish.

'Not in the least,' said Lord Werth.

'Well, that has never stopped us before,' said Gussie.

'I am flattered by your concern.'

'It *is* an urgent matter,' agreed Lady Werth. 'Though I own I would prefer not to have to go haring off after yet another Book, not two hours into our sojourn in London.'

'It was awfully careless of Mr. Ballantine to lose the thing,' said Gussie.

She had found her aunt and uncle engaged in going over the house, perhaps revisiting chambers that had once been familiar. She had discovered them in the book-room, an informal chamber too small to deserve the name of library. No fires had yet been lit, and the room languished under a settled, bone-deep chill, attended by a strong, musty odour.

These things did not appear to discompose Lord and Lady Werth in the least.

'What exactly is it you would like me to do?' said Lord Werth, leaning with one arm upon the mantelpiece. 'The Runners have the matter in hand.'

'I should suppose them perfectly capable of locating the Book,' Gussie agreed. 'But once they do, you can imagine the results, cannot you?'

Lord Werth's mouth became a grim line. 'Gussie, none of us is a match for those Books. Not now. The difference is, Mr. Ballantine's men are professionals. *We* are bystanders.'

'Or we would very much like to be,' put in Lady Werth, from her position by one long, fogged window. She was gazing out into the street, and did not turn.

'If by "professionals" you mean they are being paid to be slaughtered in the street by a Book *we* created—'

'*We* did no such thing,' interrupted Lord Werth. 'What a single, long-ago ancestor of ours may have done is of no particular relevance now.'

'Uncle.' Gussie folded her arms. 'You know as well as I do that we are the *only* ones who stand any chance of overcoming Mrs. Daventry's curse-book.'

'I know no such thing. Mr. Ballantine's Runners are specialists in Wyrded, er, situations—'

'But not this one. You heard Mr. Ballantine.'

'And if I may remind you, *our* Book almost killed you.'

'But it did not.'

Lord Werth regarded his niece with a look both irritated and puzzled. 'Did you tell me what it is you want me to do? I don't recall.'

'I want you to raise Mother Ave out of her grave.'

This brought Lady Werth from the window. 'What?' said she, turning swiftly about. 'Gussie, no. Your uncle is not fully recovered from his efforts at Starminster, not to mention from the shock of events at the Towers — and his leg requires rest!'

'There will be plenty of time for that later. Come, it will hardly take any time at all! A morning's work, and we will all sit down to a comfortable dinner with the whole sorry business behind us.'

'Do you happen to know where Avice Haye is buried?'

181

interjected Lord Werth.

'No, but Mr. Ballantine might. His men have uncovered virtually everything about her life; why not her death, too?'

'What good will it do?' said Lady Werth. 'She is responsible for the curse laid on *us*. She had nothing to do with the creation of those Books.'

'No, but the extent and strength of said curse proves that she is extraordinarily powerful, or she was when she was alive. If anyone can deal with those things, it must be her.'

'Cannot we just burn the thing, like the last one?' said Lady Werth, in some exasperation.

'With similar results?' said Gussie. 'The Book of Werth amplified Lord Felix's fire. You know it did. It *deliberately* burned the Towers, in an act of admittedly delicious revenge; what will Mrs. Daventry's curse-book do to London?'

Lord Werth was heard to sigh.

'*Besides*, do we think Ademar Wirt and his nasty little band stopped at fashioning a mere three Books? I doubt it. There will be more out there. Are we going to try to burn them all, or would we like a neater solution?'

'Ademar Wirt burned Avice Haye alive,' said Lady Werth. 'Why would she help his descendants?'

Gussie's smile was sly. 'Because her curse has been remarkably effective, has it not? We are every bit as Wyrde as she was.'

Lord Werth, having capitulated, made an ill-advised attempt to persuade Gussie to stay at home. This was about as successful as any reasonable person would expect. 'If my aunt goes,' said Gussie stubbornly, 'we all go.'

And Lady Werth *was* going. Not without protest, and not even Gussie was incapable of experiencing some small flicker of compulsion upon beholding her aunt's evident weariness. But Lady Werth said, 'If there *is* to be any burning, you will want to have me along,' and since this was inarguable, it was a reluctant but dauntless quartet that set forth from the house in Hanover Place (Great-Aunt Honoria, too, refusing to be excluded). Only Miss Frostell remained behind at the house, with a dozing Great-Uncle Silvester perched atop the door into the book-room.

The coach, only just put away, was called out again, and the horses put-to, for the (mercifully much shorter) journey to Bow-Street.

'I never saw a fifteenth-century corpse raised before,' said Great-Aunt Honoria's head, from its position atop Gussie's knee. 'What a treat.'

'Yes, you have,' said Gussie. 'You saw my uncle raise Lady Muriel Selwyn over Christmas.'

'Oh! So I did. She was excessively decayed.' This reflection pleased her enormously, for she subsided into a contented silence, smiling over the visions her memory conjured up.

'Avice Haye is probably buried in Gloucester,' said Lord Werth grumpily.

'Then we have a long trip ahead of us,' said Gussie.

The more urgent problem, upon arrival in Bow-Street, was the whereabouts of Mr. Ballantine.

'He isn't here,' came the answer, when Lord Werth had finally managed to accost somebody to ask. The Runners' headquarters was virtually devoid of people, and those few who remained were enormously busy. The only reason *this* fellow had not gone out with his colleagues was because he was too fat to chase after the curse-book, or so Gussie supposed from looking at him. Nor was he especially good-natured, for he frowned at Lord Werth, and tried to push past the entourage blocking the passage.

'Wait a moment, please,' said Gussie. 'Do you know where we can find him? It really is terribly important.' She tried the effects of a charming smile upon the rumpled and out-of-breath Runner.

'I do not,' came the short and unhelpful answer.

'Well then, do *you* know where Avice Haye, or Old Mother Ave, is buried?'

He stared. 'I beg your pardon?'

'My uncle would like to talk to her,' she explained.

The fat Runner glanced sideways at Lord Werth. Her uncle looked innocuous enough at first glance; impressions of his nature, and perhaps his consequence, were rapidly being revised.

'You must be the Werths,' said the Runner after a moment.

Great-Aunt Honoria's head gave its cackling laugh. 'Really, my good fellow, and what gave it away?'

'Wait a moment,' said the Runner, and hastened off down the passage.

'What a discourteous fellow,' said Lady Werth, without much rancour.

'There is a state of emergency presently prevailing, Aunt,' Gussie pointed out. 'He is probably not having a very good day.'

The Runner returned after about five minutes, and he bore with him a sheaf of papers rather ragged about the edges. These he thrust into Lord Werth's grasp. 'Henshawe's findings,' he said briefly, and departed again.

No one tried to stop him, this time; all were intent upon the papers Lord Werth held.

'Henshawe must be the man Mr. Ballantine sent to Gloucester,' Gussie said. 'What has he put here, Uncle?'

'Is Mother Ave's burial place conveniently written down?' said Lady Werth, with distant interest.

Lord Werth leafed through a few papers, and then passed several of them to Gussie. 'No,' he finally concluded.

Lady Werth's smile was wintry.

'Hardly surprising,' said Great-Aunt Honoria. 'If she was burned at the stake, there would not be much left, would there?'

'And whatever bones remained would likely be hurled

into a mass burial pit,' added Lady Werth.

Gussie, suffering under disappointment and chagrin, said nothing.

'But,' said Lord Werth slowly, handing another page to Gussie. 'There may be an alternative.'

Gussie, looking at the spot he indicated, drew in a gasp of air. 'Ademar Wirt!'

'Thought to have died in London,' said Lord Werth. 'Perhaps we can find him.'

'Excellent!' said Lady Werth. 'Let us search the entire city for a grave that must be a few centuries old. I have no doubt that an intact set of remains is to be found in it, and that we can complete this exciting project by tea-time.'

'I cannot see how he would help us,' said Great-Aunt Honoria. 'Those Books are doing exactly what he wanted them to do.'

'He could be persuaded to help us,' growled Gussie.

'A delightfully violent prospect,' nodded Great-Aunt Honoria.

'No,' said Lady Werth. 'Gussie, I commend your enthusiasm, but your aunt is right. Even if we could find this Mr. Wirt, he has no reason in the world to help us to dismantle his own creations. Not only would it be a waste of our time to attempt it, but I am persuaded any results we may be able to get will come too late anyway.'

Gussie paced a few steps, and back again. 'I cannot disagree with what you say,' she allowed.

Lady Werth appeared startled, and well she might. Ready capitulation from Gussie was no common event.

'I have two notions to propose,' Gussie continued.

Lady Werth visibly braced herself. 'Go on.'

'One, is that we continue to pursue this "project", as you put it, even if it is to take too long to be of any use regarding Mrs. Daventry's curse-book.'

'But—' began Lady Werth.

'It can wait until after tea,' Gussie said.

'*And* a night's rest,' insisted Lady Werth.

'It can wait until next week, for all I care. With two of the known Books gone, and the third already on the rampage, it can hardly matter *when* we resolve this mystery. I only hope we can do so before any more Books emerge.'

Lady Werth inclined her head. 'Very well. And the other notion?'

'We burn Mrs. Daventry's curse-book.'

'Did you not *just* say that to do so would be to burn half of London?'

'I did, but I cannot now recall why this struck me as an insuperable obstacle.' She beamed at her aunt, and added, 'Besides, we have the Queen of Winter with us.'

Lady Werth looked blank.

'That is you, Aunt.'

'You just wanted to go grave-robbing,' Great-Aunt Honoria surmised.

Gussie blinked. 'What lively and intelligent young woman would not?'

'The thing must be destroyed,' said Lord Werth, doggedly returning to the subject at hand. 'Burning is the only method known to be effective.'

'Shame we did not bring Lord Felix,' put in Great-Aunt Honoria. 'It is too late to go back for him, I suppose?'

'We have no need of Lord Felix,' said Gussie. 'Even a candle should be enough.'

But before this promising theme could be developed any further, Mr. Ballantine himself strode into the Bow-Street office, and happened upon the Werth quartet mid-debate.

Gussie stopped in the middle of a sentence, surprised beyond speech, for three different reasons.

For one thing, Mr. Ballantine looked *different*. It was the tusks that did it, and the bulk, and the horns; Gussie's first glimpse of the Runner in his Wyrded state proved profoundly startling.

For another thing, in addition to his transformed state he was also looking the worse for wear. More specifically, the state of his long coat and his red waist-coat and his hair suggested that somebody had lately attempted to incinerate him.

And the third thing?

'What the Devil are you all doing in here?' said Lord Bedgberry, striding along in Mr. Ballantine's wake, his thunderous countenance proclaiming him splendidly out of temper. He, too, looked fresh from an argument with a torch, or possibly with Lord Felix.

Gussie found her voice. 'Good to see you are still with us, cousin.'

Theo paused. 'Good to see *you* are still with us, come to think of it, but that don't answer my question.'

'We are here to burn the Book,' said Gussie.

Mr. Ballantine held up the scorched remains of something that had once possessed such assorted accoutrements as thick vellum pages, a leather cover, and silver hinges. 'This Book?'

Gussie stared. Nobody made a sound, in fact, save for Great-Aunt Honoria, who laughed so hard she fell into a fit of wheezing.

'Well!' said Gussie, collecting herself. 'You have managed the thing very neatly. I commend you.'

'Not exactly,' said Mr. Ballantine sourly. 'Half of Drury Lane is ablaze.'

SEVENTEEN

Theo's journey back to London easily ranked among his least favourite ever. Not that he had travelled especially often, but that did not matter. A worse trip could scarcely be imagined. A sensation perilously close to alarm, but which he refused to term anything of the sort, kept him on edge throughout the day, and since the need for haste had prompted him to urge his driver on to all possible speed, his progress towards London was the bouncing, jolting, rattling sort that left him with a strong headache.

He did not dwell upon the possible fate of his mother, father and cousin. Lord Bedgberry was simply not the type to fret himself into a stew, or to fall into a decline. But the effort of not doing so could only contribute to his discomfort.

He did not choose to stop to rest, but travelled the night through, and on into the morning. Had he but known it, his arrival at the Towers had missed the departure of his family by a scant few hours; as such, when his chaise went a-rattling and a-juddering over the London roads, and bore him inexorably towards Bow Street, his mother and father were at that moment peacefully taking tea in Hanover Place (Gussie's impetuous dash after mouldering medieval corpses as yet still brewing in her over-excited breast).

Theo did not make it to the Bow-Street office.

He *nearly* did. But something happened; one of those strange quirks of fate that sometimes occur, and leave those involved scratching their heads until long after the event.

No sooner had his driver turned the chaise into Drury Lane than it came to an abrupt halt, thanks to a resounding — but not entirely catastrophic — impact. Theo, tossed about inside, heard horses shrieking, and several people shouting.

He shoved open the door, and half fell out of the chaise — just in time to see a familiar object streaking across the pavement. As might be anticipated, it had pages and hinges and a cover, etc, and yes, of course it was Mrs. Daventry's curse-book.

To Theo, this came as an utter surprise, and for fully ten seconds he stood frozen, utterly flabbergasted.

During this period, the enterprising Book (proceeding at a dead run, thanks to the three furred feet it had apparently purloined from the steel chest) crossed from one side of the street to the other, taking a hearty bite out of two or three hapless bystanders along the way, and proposed to disappear into a grand building opposite.

Theo also had time to perceive two men — Runners, by their red waist-coats — pounding along in pursuit.

'Oh no, you don't,' growled Theo, and hurled himself after the lot of them.

Mrs. Daventry's curse-book couldn't half run; this became clear after about fifteen seconds more. Whether that third leg gave it a fifty percent advantage over Theo's two, or whether some other, eldritch force lent it an unholy speed, Theo could not tell. He only knew that he, and the two Runners, pounded along in its wake without gaining upon it at all.

Some unfortunate gentleman came out of the grand

building in question at precisely the wrong moment. Mrs. Daventry's curse-book leaped, snarling, and the gentleman fell in a wetly red heap.

This occurrence did have the advantage of deflecting the Book, however, for instead of disappearing inside the building, it darted sideways and streaked away down an adjacent alley instead.

'It is a dead end!' Theo shouted, upon reaching the mouth of the alley. 'We've got it!'

Or so he hoped; he would not have been excessively surprised to see the resourceful thing sprout wings, and fly off.

But it did not. It ran until it encountered a sheer wall, rather taller than Theo was himself. No wings appeared, nor did it, somehow, climb; it skulked instead at the base, snarling and muttering something.

As Theo drew closer, he heard what that something was.

'Thou Shalt Rive into small Parts all those Called to the Wyrde.'

'Well, that would be me,' Theo said, coming to a halt a few feet in front of it. He bared his throat, his lips drawing up into a snarl. 'Take your chance, then.'

'Sir,' came the voice of a Runner directly behind him. 'You had better move out of the way. Slowly, now.'

'Don't interfere,' said Theo shortly.

'Sir—' began the Runner again, and Theo felt himself shoved aside.

Cursing at the fumbling incompetency of Ballantine's men, Theo caught his balance and hurled himself at the curse-book. 'See what you have made me do,' he shouted, engaged at once in a violent battle for supremacy. 'I wanted it to come to *me,* but no! Oh no, what must the Runners do but *interfere*—' Here he was obliged to leave off, for a clinging and stinging appendage fastened itself over his face in a passable attempt to throttle him.

Theo paused to rip the thing away, resigning himself to

the fact that some portion of his skin must perforce go with it. '*Ouch*,' he bellowed, more in irritation than in pain, and then: 'Either of you happen to have any fire about you?'

Nobody answered him.

'Plenty of time!' he gasped, as another appendage wound around his throat. 'No hurry at all!'

'Out of the way!' came a new voice, recognisably Ballantine's. Something bright flared in Theo's vision: some manner of torch, wielded by Ballantine himself, and luxuriously aflame.

With a final, herculean effort, Theo tore the curse-book away from him and hurled it to the ground.

Ballantine, all muscles and tusks, threw himself down after it, torch in hand.

It was not long before the brittle, dry pages of Mrs. Daventry's curse-book caught, and began to smoke.

'I heard that burning's effective,' panted the Runner. Theo was already down on the cold and icy cobblestones of the alley, grimly holding the Book in place as Ballantine applied the fire to its covers. 'The only thing known to work, but we *must* contain it—'

Theo's only response to that was a short bark of incredulous laughter, and none too soon, for once the curse-book was fairly ablaze it proved impossible to hold onto any longer — not if he preferred to retain the use of his hands.

He clung grimly to it until the pain in his fingers and his arms grew too great; and then he let go.

The curse-book made a frenzied dash for the mouth of the alley. Both of Ballantine's men lunged for it; the Book responded by emitting a great *gust* of flame, as though it had exhaled a huge quantity of air all in a rush; and this measure having successfully repelled the Runners, it made it as far as the wider street, and disappeared.

Theo, a particularly filthy curse falling from his lips, ran after it.

There was no catching the curse-book a second time. Once the frenzy of its imminent demise was upon it, and presumably an accompanying desire for vengeance, Mrs. Daventry's curse-book ran so far, and so fast, that no one could get anywhere near it.

After ten minutes' magnificent rampage up and down Drury Lane, which left a quantity of buildings, carriages and people on fire, the curse-book quite literally burned itself out.

Theo, trailing doggedly in its approximate wake, even if he could not catch it, witnessed the moment of its final collapse. How it had managed to go on as more and more of it burned away was rather impressive; really, it was a pity the things were so unmanageable, for they were undoubtedly a marvel of Wyrde-work.

Only once fully three-quarters of the curse-book had turned to ash did the thing keel over. It lay in a pitiful, still-smoking heap in the middle of Drury Lane, surrounded by the wreckage it had wrought, its three ridiculous legs reduced to a single one, still twitching.

Theo, with a grunt of pain, bent over and picked it up. This, too, hurt, but he insisted upon carrying the remains out of the way of the fires before he let go of it. Who knew but what the infernal thing might yet be capable of a revival, as improbable as it seemed. If that should come to pass, Theo wanted it where he could see it.

It did not, however. An hour later, when the fires set up and down Drury Lane proved impossible to control, Theo and Ballantine had judged it wisest to take the miscreant responsible for them away from the scene, and restore it to an alternative prison. 'Where it had better be reduced to ash entirely,' Theo said grimly.

'The thing is as good as done,' said Ballantine. His face was drawn and tense, partly with pain, perhaps also with regret. Theo knew he blamed himself for the fires, and all the damage they were doing; what he thought he could have done to contain the Book while it burned, Theo could not have said. Setting it alight had been a gamble, one which they had resoundingly lost.

That said, he could not have suggested any other way of destroying, or disabling, the curse-book which was at all likely to work. God knew he had attempted virtually every conceivable method in recent years, and found none of them lastingly effective. Very few were even temporarily effective.

'I imagine I would have done the same,' Theo said generously. 'In your shoes.'

'Thank you,' said Mr. Ballantine, rather shortly.

Theo subsided into faintly injured silence.

After a few minutes of weary trudging, Ballantine sighed. 'I wish there had been some other way.'

'There wasn't. Take it from me.'

'Or that we could do *something* about the fires. The fire officers are totally overmatched.'

'Pity my mother is not here,' said Theo.

Mr. Ballantine looked at him. 'What could she do?'

'Ice.'

'On that scale?'

'I haven't a notion, but perhaps she might.'

Some few minutes later they entered the Bow-street office, finding Lord and Lady Werth, Great-Aunt Honoria, and Gussie cluttering up the passage not far from the front door.

After the conversation already related, Theo said, 'Mother, just the person wanted. Do you think you could do something?'

'Take me there,' said she. 'Gussie, Honoria, you had better stay here.'

'But—'

'I am sure it will be dangerous.'

'Perhaps we could help.'

'How?'

Gussie visibly groped for a sensible answer. 'Buckets of

water… Great-Aunt Honoria could pour water from above! Like she did at the Towers.'

'The fire's well beyond that,' said Mr. Ballantine. 'Miss Werth, I should be grateful for your assistance with this.' He held up the scorched remains of Mrs. Daventry's curse-book.

'What do you propose to do to it?' said Gussie.

'Burn what is left of it, and then bury the ash as deep down as I can get.'

Gussie's smile was the sort to strike terror into the hearts of innocents. 'Oh, *yes*,' she breathed. 'I should be delighted to help you with *that*.'

Lady Werth's work on Drury Lane inspired in her son a new respect for her abilities.

The journey from Bow Street was but a short one. With every step her ladyship took, fresh layers of frost coated her skin; ice-crystals glinted in her hair; her face gradually turned a stark snow-white, and winter blossomed in her eyes.

By the time they reached the edges of the conflagration, she was winter incarnate. Indeed, one unlucky bystander, happening to pass too close to her ladyship, became an ice-sculpture upon the spot.

'Oops,' said Lady Werth absently, in a hailstorm of a voice.

'You can send a note of apology later,' said Theo.

'With one of those nice ices from Gunter's,' said Lady Werth.

'That ought to make up for it,' Theo agreed. 'Though it is just possible the lady might have had enough of ice, whenever she should thaw.'

Lady Werth waved off this reflection, being now intent upon the fires greedily decimating Drury Lane. She paused in observation for some few moments, while Theo stood at her side, trying to ignore the conflagration of pain in his own, sadly burned hands, and growing more impatient by the second.

'Mother—' he began at last. 'I hate to rush you, but did you happen to notice that the street is on fire?'

Her only response was a withering look.

Then she took in a deep, fortifying breath, and the frost liberally coating her own, neat form began to spread.

It shot up the cobbled street before her in a thick, unstoppable wave, quenching every lick of flame it encountered.

Once it reached the burning buildings, it became a blizzard of stinging ice, beyond which point, Theo could discern little of what occurred, for the vast gusts of steam sent up obscured most of the scene.

Lady Werth walked slowly, inexorably forward, her husband at her back and her son at her side (not that Theo had the smallest notion what he might do for her, but Lord Bedgberry understood his duty — and on this one, rare occasion was actually willing to perform it). Everywhere she stepped, fresh sheets of ice erupted, and rattled into battle.

The hungry fires put up a tolerable fight — indeed, one enterprising inferno did its best to swallow Lady Werth and Theo both, at one exciting moment — but nothing much can survive winter, and the fire of Drury Lane proved no exception. Some half an hour saw the end of the sorry business, and if there was a degree of collateral damage incurred in the process, well, that was of little moment. Anyone who objected too strongly to finding their theatre become a block of ice ought to reflect on how much less they would like to find it a pile of ash.

The fate of the those trapped by the flames — or standing by to gawp — was something of a shame, but they, too, would thaw eventually.

As would Lady Werth, who, exhausted by her (admittedly spectacular) efforts achieved two distinct changes in her state.

The first was her inevitable alteration into a delicate

statue of herself, wrought in ice; common enough, whenever her ladyship was put under intolerable pressure.

The second was her sinking into a deep swoon, in the very moment of her transformation; *this* being very unusual indeed.

Theo, having with admirable presence of mind foreseen this danger, and rushed to interrupt his mother's descent towards an unforgiving ground, found himself burned for the second time that morning — this time with ice.

He swore, and let Lady Werth fall the rest of the way to the pavement.

'Sorry,' he said awkwardly, as she lay there insensate, and his father gave an irritable sigh. 'But my hands hurt like the *blazes*.'

EIGHTEEN

The remnants of Mrs. Daventry's ill-fated curse-book made for a pitiful pile of ash, when it came down to it.

Gussie and Mr. Ballantine — and Great-Aunt Honoria, apparently far more interested in the setting of fires than the extinguishing of them — took the charred and smoking fragment out into a yard at the back of the Bow-street office, rather than attempting a final burning of it inside. 'For,' as Gussie pointed out, 'if the thing should take it into its head to revive at the crucial moment, your charming headquarters would be toast by tea-time.'

Mr. Ballantine, still mightily ogrish, took charge of keeping the Book in its appointed spot, while Gussie set the fire. She had a tinderbox, and all the aid Great-Aunt Honoria's head could give her by way of hearty puffs upon every spark that materialised.

Since Honoria inevitably blew many of them out before they had time to catch, the process of setting the stub of the Book alight took some minutes. Gussie spent all of them with one eye on the tinderbox and one upon the Book itself, expecting every moment to see an ominous stirring of its pages, or the beginnings of one of its abominable appendages slithering out from between the covers.

But nothing of the sort occurred. Within ten short minutes, she had a merry blaze going, and Mr. Ballantine judged it safe to cautiously withdraw his hold upon it.

The three of them stood — or, in Great-Aunt Honoria's case, floated — in a desultory ring around the burning Book, watching in a sort of sickened fascination as the troublesome thing burned up once and for all.

When all that was left was a faintly smoking pool of ash, Mr. Ballantine gave something of a sigh. Gussie thought it the sound of a man mentally relinquishing a burden he'd had no choice but to carry for some time.

'And good riddance!' declared Great-Aunt Honoria, performing a frenzied victory dance in mid-air. She may not even have meant to leak blood all over the ashy remains.

At some point, Gussie became aware that Mr. Ballantine's gaze had transferred to her, and there remained fixed.

She met that gaze, with a look both questioning and perhaps challenging.

Mr. Ballantine proved either unwilling or unable to explain what he meant by it.

'Oh!' said Gussie, a moment's reflection elucidating his conduct. 'Is it the tusks you are concerned about?'

Mr. Ballantine touched one of the tusks in question, with a look of mild chagrin. 'They aren't pretty, after all.'

'You expected me to evince signs of disquiet, perhaps? Disgust?'

'I am accustomed to it. Especially from the fairer sex.'

This comment, for some reason, sent Great-Aunt Honoria off into gales of laughter.

'Don't I disgust you?' Mr. Ballantine pressed.

'Why should you?'

Mr. Ballantine appeared startled.

'Though I can perfectly understand why my opinion should weigh with you,' Gussie added, nodding wisely.

'Being a jewel among said fairer sex, after all — a paragon of womanhood, not to mention a diamond of the first water — why, no reasonable man could be expected to *live* with my disapprobation.'

This, paradoxically, Great-Aunt Honoria did not appear to find amusing at all. 'Quite right,' she said, with a brisk nod. 'There is an occasional man as has a modicum of sense.'

Mr. Ballantine smiled at that. 'I've never seen another like me,' he said simply.

'Even with your job?' Gussie said, with interest. 'How rare a specimen you are.'

'I am that.'

'Come to think of it, so am I. Do I seem a monster to you?'

'Utterly, and beyond all hope of redemption,' said Mr. Ballantine promptly.

'I believe I shall like you quite as well as Lord Maundevyle,' Gussie said, well pleased. 'Perhaps even more! Who can tell?'

Mr. Ballantine chuckled, in the fashion Gussie was beginning to like. In his... amplified state, his usual laughter had gained an extra depth, a rumbling timbre rather pleasing than otherwise to the ear. 'That puts me in mind of something,' he said, but then hesitated, rather than simply say it outright, as any man of sense and daring would do.

'Well, what is it?' said Gussie.

'I ought first to consult with one or two people.'

'Before you do what?'

'Before I risk an earful by laying my idea before you.'

'A rare specimen, but a cowardly one,' Gussie pronounced.

Mr. Ballantine held up both hands. 'Now, now. A degree of caution has its place in life, you know.'

'I know nothing of the sort.'

'And if you should dislike the scheme, I'd as lief not

give you an opportunity to flay me alive unnecessarily. It may yet come to nothing, after all.'

'You intrigue me in spite of myself.'

'I shan't leave you in suspense for long,' Mr. Ballantine promised. 'Now, then. We had best get that mess cleaned up, before I go and find out how your excellent aunt is getting on in Drury Lane.'

'She will be somewhat the worse for wear, I expect. Wintering on that sort of scale cannot be good for her.' She stirred the pile of ashes with the toe of her shoe. 'Where shall we bury this?'

'Hallowed ground?' suggested Mr. Ballantine.

'I am not perfectly sure that the things are genuinely infernal, but by all means. It cannot hurt.'

Gussie had prophesied truly, as she soon discovered, for poor Lady Werth was borne back into Hanover Place in the arms of a pair of stout footmen, and set down upon the bed in one of the most comfortable bedchambers. An expanse of waxed cloth was first laid down, in case her ladyship should melt as she lay there. Gussie and Great-Aunt Honoria saw that the room was swept free of dust and properly cleaned by the maids, and with their own hands (or Gussie's, at least, under her great-aunt's direction) adorned the room with vases of passably attractive silk flowers. She also laid two or three novels by her aunt's bedside. 'In case she should feel bored, when she thaws,' Gussie explained.

'She will feel ravenously hungry, and is like to make straight for the kitchen,' Great-Aunt Honoria said.

Spurred by which happy thought, Gussie also instructed that a glass of wine and a plate of cakes should be taken up to her aunt's bedside every two hours, until such time as she should wake.

With these arrangements made, she set about settling in at Hanover Place, with all the unpacking and shopping and what-not that this entailed. Lord Werth preferring to shut himself in the book-room, with a good fire and a quantity of improving reading, Gussie also took care of her aunt's chambers, and bought for her a spectacular bonnet she saw in a shop in Bond Street, and could not resist purchasing. It had a very wide brim, was upholstered in an exciting shade of red, and sported an effusion of cleverly fashioned butterflies bursting from the crown.

Theo required the constant attendance of a doctor, for a few days, for the extent of his burns proved rather greater than anybody had realised. Perhaps something of strain and shock had got to him, too, however little he liked to admit it, for he lay in bed for three days together, feverish and sick, and by the time he felt well enough to leave it Gussie had proceeded so far as to *think* about feeling some concern over him.

Once fairly out of his bed, he joined his father in the book-room, and the two of them were but little seen for the rest of the week.

'They will be talking over the rebuilding of the Towers,' said Great-Aunt Honoria wisely. 'The work will begin in the spring, no doubt.'

Gussie did not have to wait all that long for an explanation of Mr. Ballantine's mysterious conduct, after all. On the fourth day after the fires, when Theo had risen and shut himself into the book-room, and Lady Werth had revived enough to drink tea, Mr. Ballantine called at the house, and asked for Miss Werth.

She joined him in the parlour, with a merry smile and a hearty welcome. 'I had begun to think you had forgotten.'

'It hasn't been so very long, surely?' he protested, making his bow.

'To a woman living in a fever of suspense, every minute seems an hour.

He was his normal self again, or at least the version of himself with which Gussie was most familiar; who knew which state felt more natural to him? 'Well, but I come with an entreaty,' said he. 'Those with whom I have consulted were in total agreement with me.'

'As to what?' said Gussie, waving him to a chair, and taking one herself.

'That the abilities enjoyed by the Wyrded could be of great use to the Runners.'

'Enjoyed?' said Gussie. 'Or endured?'

'One or the other. See, many of my fellow Runners are Wyrded, like myself, but many more are not. Now, I have found my own Wyrde to be of more than passing convenience—'

'I should imagine so,' murmured Gussie.

'—and Lady Werth has just demonstrated the value of hers, very ably indeed,' he went on, paying no heed to Gussie's interjection save a slight smile. 'Even Lord Felix's, properly directed, could be invaluable.'

'Wielded by someone retaining some faint vestiges of sanity, do you mean?'

'More or less that, yes.'

'I can see where I am to come in,' said Gussie.

Mr. Ballantine nodded.

'You want me to paw all the non-Wyrded Runners in Bow Street, in hopes of spawning a dragon or two.'

'Shall you mind the idea?'

'Perhaps more importantly, shall they? I did not speak entirely idly, when I mentioned endurance. Not everybody is as well-pleased with their Wyrde as you seem to be.'

'It would not be conducted against anybody's will,' Mr. Ballantine said quickly.

'And I am glad to hear it, but nonetheless. It is difficult to know what one is letting oneself in for, especially as the Wyrde is so capricious. I need only think of my poor Aunt Wheldrake, her heart irrevocably set on her daughter's turning daintily mermaid, and obliged to put up with a gorgon in her place.'

Mr. Ballantine chuckled. 'I think I can promise that my men will be hoping for more of that sort of an outcome. To be a gorgon, now. For a Runner, that would be something.'

'And the Wyrde being what it is, they are as like to end up as mermaids instead.'

'Which would be no terrible result, either. That kind of aptitude in water could be of great value.'

Gussie pursed her lips, unconvinced.

'Never tell me you are concerned for my men's welfare,' said Mr. Ballantine. 'That does not sound like Miss Werth at all.'

'My concern,' said Gussie coolly, 'is for my own hide, Mr. Ballantine, and that of my family.'

'That sounds more likely,' he agreed.

'If some of these subordinates of yours decide they are unhappy with the transformation, at whom do you suppose they will direct their ire? At you? Or at me?'

'I will ensure they know at whose door to lay the responsibility.'

'That being yours,' Gussie said,

'Absolutely and entirely mine.'

'Well, then,' said Gussie. 'I *have* been feeling a little bored, since the events of Drury Lane. My aunt has not been in a fit state to go out, you see, and my uncle and my cousin will hardly show themselves outside of the book-room.'

'Then we will have a pleasant jaunt down to Bow Street, someday soon,' he promised.

'I have a condition,' Gussie said.

'By all means, name it. In fact, I consider myself in your debt anyway, or your family's. Without your help, the curse-book would still be on the rampage, and we'd have lost half of London's theatre district.'

'Excellent,' said Gussie brightly. 'Then I should like to join Bow Street.'

He stared, and blinked. 'Join—?'

'I want to become a Runner, Mr. Ballantine.'

'You… of course you do.'

'Come, now, I would make an excellent Runner. I have

courage, wit, and energy, not to mention a knowledge and experience of the Wyrde virtually unparalleled in England. I would be an asset to your division.'

Poor Mr. Ballantine coughed, and struggled for a moment to form suitable words. '….Ah, I am afraid to tell you, Miss Werth, that despite your many qualifications it won't be in my power to grant you a place in my division.'

'And why not?'

Mr. Ballantine hesitated.

'You are going to tell me that women are not allowed, aren't you?'

'That is about the size of it, yes.'

'Nonsense. Just because there have been no women before, does not mean there cannot be any now.'

He groped for more words. 'There… there are none of the arrangements that would be necessary, for a female Runner—'

'Such as what?'

Mr. Ballantine mumbled something about the comfort of ladies.

'Is it because I am an aristocrat?' she demanded. 'I will renounce my rarefied blood on the spot, if it would help.'

Mr. Ballantine sighed, and rubbed at his eyes. 'I am afraid the answer has to be no,' he said. 'Anything else I may do for you is done in an instant, but that I cannot grant.'

'I will carry my point eventually,' she warned him.

'I have the paralysing fear that you might,' he agreed.

Pleased with this idea, she smiled winsomely at him. 'In that case, I will have to act as a Runner on my own account, and without official backing.'

'You—'

'You may help me with that, if you please. I want to find Ademar Wirt's grave, and, with my uncle's help, question him.'

'Dare I ask to what end?'

'I am persuaded there must be more of those Books

somewhere in the world, and when they show up, we would like to be better prepared, would not we? We cannot go about burning down half of England in an attempt to keep up with them.'

'And you think Ademar Wirt will tell you all about them? Together with a neat list of instructions as to how to disable them?'

'People will do all kinds of uncharacteristic things, if suitable pressure is applied.'

Mr. Ballantine stared at her in a kind of dull horror.

'As I said before,' said Gussie triumphantly, 'I would make an excellent Runner.'

Mr. Ballantine took a long swallow of tea, and set down his cup with a crash. 'God help us all.'

The process of rendering Mr. Ballantine's unfortunate colleagues Wyrded proved a simple one. Gussie presented herself at Bow Street early in the morning two days after the conversation related above, attended by Theo — at his insistence rather than hers.

'Dash it, cousin, you cannot walk unattended into a room full of Bow Street Runners!' said he, when she mentioned her errand.

'This is what comes of not allowing women to join,' said Gussie wisely. 'Though why it should make a difference I couldn't say. They are only *men*.'

Theo glowered. 'Men who are shortly to turn Wyrded, thanks to your excellent efforts. Who knows what they may do *then*?'

'Now I comprehend,' said Gussie, nodding. 'Really, I *could* not imagine that you were in a stew over propriety.'

'There is a danger! I shall have to go with you.'

'We do not know that any of them will be in the smallest degree altered,' she pointed out. 'If they lack the capacity, I may maul them as I choose, and they shall remain perfectly ordinary. Like Clarissa Selwyn.'

'Perfectly true; or they might all of them turn into ogres

on the spot, and you will be crushed to death in the ensuing stampede. I shall go with you.'

'Really, Theo, have a care. I shall begin to develop the idea that you are interested in my welfare.'

'Nothing of the sort,' said Theo shortly. 'If you should be brought home in pieces, I shall never hear the end of it from Mother.'

'Yes; nobody knows how to fetch Lady Werth's shawl quite like I do.'

'Even Father would be somewhat displeased, I imagine.'

'And Great-Aunt Honoria would haunt you for eternity.'

That prospect was enough to make him blanch; his eyes started in horror. 'Talking, and talking, and *talking!* Good God! That decides it. We will attend upon Mr. Ballantine together, or— or—'

'Or what?' said Gussie, interested.

'Or— I shall be forced to lock you in your room.'

Gussie's eyes widened slightly. 'Oh, no. I *quake* with terror.'

'And how should you go to Bow Street *then*, I should like to know?'

'Great-Aunt Honoria would let me out.'

Theo cursed.

'What abominable language.'

Theo was as good as his word, however. The above exchange took place very late on the morning after Mr. Ballantine's visit, finding a sleepy-eyed Lord Bedgberry still arrayed in a silk dressing gown with a pattern Gussie could only term violent. The morning after that, however, he appeared much earlier, fully dressed in respectable raiment, and if not actually bright-eyed then certainly alert enough for the demands of the morning. He fidgeted through Gussie's breakfast, casting frequent looks towards the door of the breakfast-parlour.

'If you are concerned that my aunt or uncle will come

in, you need not worry,' said Gussie calmly, taking another forkful of smoked fish. 'They have not been in the habit of rising so early.'

'You haven't told them what you mean to do, have you?'

'Why on earth would I do that?'

'That's what I thought.'

'My poor aunt would be sure to think of some excellent reason why I should not.'

'Which would not weigh with you at all.'

'No, but she might be made anxious, and really, she has had enough to put up with of late.'

'Very considerate of you.'

'Yes, isn't it?' Gussie finished her plate, dabbed at her mouth with her napkin, and rose from her chair. 'Very well; shall we go?'

Mr. Ballantine greeted them in person, almost from the moment they stepped into the Bow-street office. He was immaculately attired in a coat that Gussie suspected was new, with his customary red waist-coat underneath, and some mysterious power had restored order to his dark hair.

'Aren't you looking respectable,' Gussie commented, making her curtsey.

'I am overjoyed you should think so, Miss Werth.' He bowed. 'Lord Bedgberry. I had no notion I was to expect the pleasure of your company this morning.'

'Which is to say you aren't pleased,' said Theo, with a perfunctory bow. 'Gussie insisted.'

Gussie gasped. 'A lie! And so beautifully delivered.'

'No, no, I am not displeased,' said Mr. Ballantine. 'I daresay you're right to attend your cousin. Shall I offer you refreshment first, or are you ready to begin immediately?'

'We come fresh from the breakfast-parlour,' Gussie assured him. 'I couldn't eat another scrap, even were you to put a whole bucket of pastries before me.'

'Do they serve pastries in buckets, at Hanover Place?' Mr. Ballantine said, with a flicker of a smile. 'And I thought I was getting used to the odd ways of the gentry.'

'They do not, much to my disappointment,' said Gussie, following as Mr. Ballantine led the way out of the entrance-hall at Bow Street, and down a succession of passages. They went up one flight of stairs, and turned in at a door near at hand. The room beyond was quite large; a dining-parlour, perhaps, or something of that sort, though it had been cleared of almost all furniture. A long bench of polished oak ran along the rear wall, and the windows sported a set of handsome brocade curtains, but that was all.

Eight men in red waist-coats were lined up down the centre of the room.

'Gentlemen, may I present Miss Werth,' said Mr. Ballantine as he walked in, his footsteps echoing loudly in the sparse chamber. 'And her cousin, Lord Bedgberry.'

More curtsies and bows followed, while all eight heads turned in Gussie's direction, and regarded her with interest. Interest, and some trepidation, she thought, detecting a trace of nerves in more than one face. They were a mixed bunch, of all ages between twenty and fifty-five. All of them had the rather hard look of determined men — men capable of violence, if the occasion called for it.

Mr. Ballantine did not seem disposed to say anything more, so Gussie took charge of the situation. She walked into the centre of the room, and stationed herself before the first man in the row. He was among the younger ones, not much more than thirty or so, his chestnut hair neatly arranged, his calm grey eyes fixed upon her without much sign of emotion.

Mr. Ballantine said, from his station at her elbow, 'Mr. Gooding, Miss Werth.'

Gussie smiled. 'I am charmed to meet you, Mr. Gooding. How do you feel about the Wyrde?'

'If you can contrive to grant me a useful Wyrde-curse, I'll be strongly in favour of it.'

'Then let us both hope that I can, though as I am sure Mr. Ballantine has told you, I have no especial control over the process.'

Mr. Gooding inclined his head. 'How do *you* feel about the Wyrde, ma'am?'

Gussie's brows rose. 'Favourable,' she said after a moment's thought.

'And why is that?'

'Life would be *so* much less interesting without it.' She held out her hand; he extended his; they shook hands, gravely and with exquisite politeness. 'Best of luck, Mr. Gooding,' she said, and moved on to the next Runner.

Twenty minutes later, she had dutifully exchanged pleasantries and shaken hands with all eight of them, and was able to step back, her work complete. A critical eye swept over the whole row of them detected no signs, as yet, of any incipient transformation, and a glance at Mr. Ballantine's countenance declared him disappointed.

'Don't be cast down,' she told him. 'Lord Maundevyle took fully half an hour before he began to sprout scales, though his mother was rather quicker about it.'

'His mother?' said Mr. Ballantine. 'Did her ladyship turn dragon, too? I hadn't heard.'

'Not a dragon, mercifully. Mermaid.'

'Ah.'

'Of sorts.' Remembering Lady Maundevyle's transformed appearance, she permitted herself a small, slightly wicked smile.

'If the words were insufficient to worry me, that smile would do it,' Mr. Ballantine commented.

Theo had maintained a station at the back of the room throughout these proceedings, watching Gussie's progress down the line with a stern eye and forbidding countenance. He now came forward, and gently took hold of Gussie's arm. 'Well, cousin, if you are finished here I believe we will leave.'

'Before anybody has chance to change his mind, and wreak a terrible retribution upon poor, helpless me?' she said. 'I daresay you are right.'

They had made it almost to the door before Gussie became aware of a commotion behind her. She turned.

Mr. Gooding remained impassive and composed, untouched by the Wyrde. His next neighbour, however, was in the throes of what promised to be a spectacular transformation.

Gussie stood, critically observing this promising disaster, and said to Mr. Ballantine: 'I did mention to you the possibility of a *large* outcome?' She frowned. 'Perhaps I did forget, at that.'

'The dragon-Wyrde is not common, I understood—'

'I hope you are not particularly attached to this room,' she interrupted. 'For I do believe you have a wyvern on your hands.'

Poor Mr. Cooke was not enjoying the process very much, judging from the cries he was making, and the contortions of his tortured frame. The wings alone must have hurt, Gussie thought, as they erupted from the torn skin of his back; not to mention the talons splitting the tips of his fingers, and the teeth, two inches long at least, turning his mouth into a maw.

Panicked, he crossed the room in a galloping, stumbling stride and hurled himself, with a resounding *crash,* through the unoffending window. He didn't fall. His leathery, mustard-yellow wings caught him halfway down, and sent him soaring into the sky, a wyvern complete.

Silence fell.

Gussie pondered the quantity of shattered glass upon the floor, and the ashen countenances of the remaining seven Runners.

'You did not think it would work, did you?' she said to Mr. Ballantine.

'I *hoped,*' he replied. 'But not so… promptly, nor so

dramatically either.'

'You had better take the rest outside,' Gussie recommended. 'Who knows but what there might be a dragon amongst them, to boot.'

Mr. Ballantine followed her advice, marching his charges out into the street without further ado. Gussie, to Theo's disgust, insisted upon waiting a half-hour or so before leaving; she, of course, was curious, and wanted to witness the results of her handiwork.

'*Curious*,' said Theo with distaste. 'Have you not done enough damage already?'

'You blame me!' she said. 'How unjust! It is all done at the request of Mr. Ballantine.'

'There isn't a man alive has got a notion what he's in for, when he invites *you* to visit,' said Theo.

'I believe I shall change my name,' Gussie agreed. '*Augusta* is sadly mundane. What would you say to something more modern? *Walking Disaster* Werth, perhaps?'

'Fitting,' growled Theo. 'Only too tame.'

'Charming Catastrophe? No, you're right; I do like that better.'

'Very well, Miss Charming. Now we are going.'

'No, not yet. Look! I do believe Mr. Grey is next.' They stood at the window of the room adjoining the one with the shattered window, Gussie having agreed to that much at least. Up there, she would be safe enough from whatever happened below, but she could still watch it unfold.

From her vantage point, she received a clear view of Mr. Grey. One of the older Runners, being well into his forties at least, with a grim countenance and a world-weary air, he had checked his pocket-watch three times while Gussie stood watching. Whatever appointment he was in a hurry to get to would have to wait. 'Ah!' cried Gussie, clapping her hands together. 'He has got something along the lines of Mr. Selwyn's Wyrde, I think. How fitting! All that feral aggression will suit him perfectly.'

'A wyvern and a lycanthrope,' said Theo. 'Not a bad outcome, under the circumstances.'

Nor was it. Mr. Ballantine later declared himself satisfied, even though five out of the eight had remained unaltered.

He did not again visit in Hanover Place, declaring himself too busy. But she did receive a letter from him, or at least a share in Theo's.

Please thank Miss Werth for her assistance at Bow Street, he had written. *Mr. Cooke and Mr. Grey are well pleased. Mr. Blackwell requires some little time to grow accustomed, I believe, but I have no doubt he will come around.*

I believe you left before his Wyrding, thus you may not know of it. (True, for Mr. Blackwell's Wyrde had been slow to descend; Gussie and Theo had grown restless after another half-an-hour of nothing, and Gussie had allowed herself to be escorted home). *He has a new eye*, Mr. Ballantine continued. *Nicely positioned in the centre of his forehead. His vision being thus rather altered, he has suffered a great deal from sickness and dizziness, though I believe he is growing used to it now.*

'There,' said Theo, taking his letter back from Gussie's hands. 'You have made a man sick and miserable, and I hope you are now satisfied.'

'That being my eternal aim,' Gussie agreed. 'Though I have yet to make *you* sick and miserable, so my work is not yet done.'

'Who says you haven't?' Theo muttered, folding the letter, and putting it away.

Life at Hanover Square continued peacefully enough, after these exciting events. Lady Werth achieved a full recovery from her ice-bound state; under her direction, the town-house was very soon in an excellent condition, its damp and mildew banished, its shabby furnishings replaced with choice selections from the best of London's warehouses.

Theo's hands remained bandaged for some time, but the pain in them diminished day by day, and his feverish state did not return. Really, he was as good as new, except for a certain clumsiness — but Gussie considered this hardly an alteration from the usual.

Lord Werth was not best pleased to hear of Gussie's escapade at Bow Street.

Not that she was so foolish as to mention the matter to him. The newspapers, however, did.

One morning over breakfast, when Gussie had been so unwise as to linger over her tea, she found herself fixed by a gimlet stare from her uncle, who had but just taken his seat, and opened his newspaper.

'It seems a wyvern was seen to crash through the window of the Bow-Street Runners' office,' he said, tapping the open page before him.

'How remarkable,' murmured Gussie.

'A passer-by was injured by falling shards of glass, and if this paper is to be believed, the wyvern in question doubtless went on to devour dozens of people.'

'Doubtless,' Gussie agreed.

'You would not happen to know anything about this, Gussie?'

'Nothing at all,' Gussie said, choking on a swallow of cooling tea, and ruining her otherwise faultless composure.

Lord Werth sighed, shook his head, and in all probability uttered a silent prayer to any supernatural force listening to relieve him of Gussie at Their earliest opportunity.

Gussie thought it best to slide out of her chair, and beat a hasty retreat.

But karma is known to be a capricious mistress, and Gussie's just reward was bound, at some point, to materialise.

It came in the form of an official letter, signed by the Office of the Wyrde (a department belonging to the government, Gussie surmised, though not one she had ever heard of before).

'I must apply for a *license*!' she said, revolted, and all but threw the letter at Theo.

He sat reading in his favourite chair in the book-room. Gussie had, until the appearance of the letter, been peacefully reading a novel in *her* favourite chair, by the window, but now all her comfort was destroyed.

'Apply?' said Theo, not much interested, judging from his unimpaired concentration on the pages of his book.

'Yes! The implication being that they might not grant it!'

'Well,' said Theo, turning a page. 'Considering your display at Bow Street, you can hardly be surprised that they consider you a danger.'

'And what if they don't grant it?' said she, paying no heed to this. 'What must I do then? Cease to exist?'

Theo looked up at that, his eyes glinting with malicious amusement. 'You will have to run away with Lady Margery. But you will like living at the far end of the Alps, Gussie. Highly attractive scenery.'

He went back to his book.

Gussie, left to fume alone, contemplated hurling her own book at his head, but refrained. She was rather enjoying the novel.

As if this were not enough, another letter arrived a day or two later.

'I become popular,' Gussie marvelled, tearing it open. Nothing on earth would have induced her to admit that she did so with some trepidation.

'General Sir Robert Epworth?' she said, reading the signature. 'What on earth—'

A moment's rapid reading acquainted her with the whole.

'Ha!' she exclaimed with gusto.

'Well, what is it now?' said Theo, looking up from — as far as she could tell — the same dry tome he had been poring over yesterday.

'Here,' she said, handing over the letter.

As Theo read, his brows snapped down and further down, until he wore a forbidding scowl. 'What errant nonsense!' he proclaimed.

'Nothing of the sort!' Gussie retorted.

'A *whole campful of soldiers?*' Theo made to screw up the letter, but remembered at the last instant that it was hers, and irritably tossed it back to her. 'Has General Sir Robert Epworth lost his wits?

'He believes I can be useful,' said Gussie, smoothing out the letter. 'He is obviously a man of extraordinary discernment.'

'Useful? Useful? Turning a whole campful of soldiers into assorted examples of Wyrded disaster is *useful?*'

'Well, why not? Perhaps he is right. If we had had more fearsomely Wyrded military men at our disposal, the war with Bonaparte might have been sooner won.'

Theo's scowl had not lifted. 'And if it goes horribly wrong? Who do you imagine will be held responsible then?'

'General Sir Robert Epworth,' said Gussie promptly. 'As a military adjunct, my license is assured — so he says. If he can do that much for me, he can certainly protect me from any uncomfortable consequences.'

Theo grunted something incomprehensible.

'And once I am installed as an official adjunct to the military, even Mr. Ballantine will have to change his mind, and let me into the Runners' club,' she said triumphantly.

'I strongly doubt it,' said Theo, pouring cold water on everything as usual. 'I doubt it is even his decision to make.'

'Good point,' said Gussie, carefully folding her letter. 'I shall have to find out whose decision it is.'

'You are not going to do this, are you?' said Theo.

'Of course I am.'

'Can we not have a single moment's peace?'

Theo being in a fair way to losing his temper altogether,

Gussie attempted pacification. 'It won't be that bad,' she said. 'I might become a military hero, and then you will be pleased.'

Theo appeared incapable of speech, at least without exploding.

Gussie went out of the room, kindly patting his head as she passed. 'I shall go and tell my uncle and aunt,' she said.

Theo threw up his hands. 'By all means, do. Perhaps they can talk some sense into you.'

But given what we know of the disastrous Miss Werth, it will come as no surprise to learn that they didn't even try.

More From
Charlotte E. English

House of Werth:

Wyrde and Wayward
Wyrde and Wicked

The Tales of Aylfenhame:

Miss Landon and Aubranael
Miss Ellerby and the Ferryman
Bessie Bell and the Goblin King
Mr. Drake and My Lady Silver

www.charlotteenglish.com